BY NINA SADOWSKY

CONVINCE ME

BALLANTINE BOOKS

NEW YORK

CONVINCE ME

A NOVEL

Nina Sadowsky

Published in the United States by Ballantine Books, an imprint of Random House, a division of Penguin Random House LLC, New York.

BALLANTINE and the HOUSE colophon are registered trademarks of Penguin Random House LLC.

LIBRARY OF CONGRESS CATALOGING-IN-PUBLICATION DATA
Names: Sadowsky, Nina, author.
Title: Convince me : a novel / Nina Sadowsky.
Description: New York : Ballantine Books, [2020] |
Identifiers: LCCN 2020006142 (print) | LCCN 2020006143 (ebook) |
ISBN 9780525619901 (hardcover) | ISBN 9780525619918 (ebook)
Subjects: GSAFD: Mystery fiction.
Classification: LCC PS3619.A353 C66 2020 (print) |
LCC PS3619.A353 (ebook) | DDC 813/.6—dc23
LC record available at https://lccn.loc.gov/2020006142
LC ebook record available at https://lccn.loc.gov/2020006143

Printed in Canada on acid-free paper

randomhousebooks.com

2 4 6 8 9 7 5 3 1

FIRST EDITION

Title-page image: © iStockphoto.com

Book design by Dana Leigh Blanchette

This book is for everyone
who is sick and tired
of the fucking liars
and their fucking lies.

And is dedicated to K.M.

CONVINCE ME

CHAPTER ONE

ANNIE

I nearly died the day we met.

It was February, just over three years ago. I was in Mammoth for a ski trip with my best friend, Bella. On day one, Bella wiped out on her second run. The next morning, nursing a sore wrist and lump on her head, she said she wanted to take it easy.

When I came back to our condo from the slopes midday to check on her, she informed me she was hitching a ride back to L.A. with another friend. I couldn't really be angry. She felt like shit and wanted to go home. She volunteered to pay for her half of the rental and told me I should stay, ski, and mingle as she toted her suitcase out the door with her good hand.

I stayed. I skied. I didn't mingle; I was protecting my battered heart. A man about whom I'd been foolish enough to entertain "happily ever after" fantasies had proved to be a serial cheater. This bruising realization, just as we had neared our first anniversary, had led to Bella's suggestion of a few days in Mammoth—a girls' trip, now a solo retreat.

I tried to embrace it. I skied hard. Came back to the condo.

Braved the cold to make it out to the hot tub on the deck. Cooked and consumed huge bowls of pasta mixed with decadent, chunky lumps of butter and generous sprinkles of Parmesan cheese. I passed out early, exhausted, and slept deeply.

The day I was to drive back to Los Angeles, snow dumped on Mammoth. Big, fat lazy flakes.

I'm a California girl. First in line to get my learner's permit the day I turned fifteen and a half. So even though I'd been a (self-styled) demon of the road for twelve years, driving on snow was not in my particular wheelhouse.

Wary of the weather, I got an early start, loading my little Acura, wiping a crust of snow off the windshield, climbing into the car, and blasting the defrosters.

I pulled out cautiously. I found out later that the temperature had dropped into single digits the night before; a thick sheet of ice lay beneath the freshly falling wet snow. As soon as I accelerated, my car slid and skidded, the wheels churning uselessly for purchase. Frantically, I tried to remember what to do in a skid. *Turn into it? Away from it?*

Panicked, I stomped on the brake. The car fishtailed and spun. As the world twirled before my eyes, I heard a piercing noise and realized I was screaming. After what felt like an endless free fall, the front end of my car slammed broadside into a parked pickup truck with a horrific crash and the whine of metal greeting metal.

The airbag exploded. My head snapped back and then forward. My vision blurred. I blinked and wiped my eyes. My hand came away bloody.

But I was alive. I sat there dazed for a moment, or maybe it was an hour.

A face appeared through the splintered windshield. A man's face, kind and open, classically handsome, twisted in concern. He opened my car door and leaned in.

"I'm Justin Childs," he introduced himself. "And it looks like you might need a hand."

He's dead now, this man I came to know and love and marry.

I'm a widow.

At the tender age of thirty-one.

That fact, cold, hard, and inescapable, seems distant and absurd, like a tragedy from someone else's life, not mine.

This wasn't supposed to happen to me.

My life before Justin's death wasn't perfect. I had my fair amount of shit, like anyone else, but I was aware that I enjoyed a lot of relative privilege.

I'm white. I was blessed with appealing looks. I was raised in a solidly middle-class family. I'm well educated. My bio dad took off when I was a baby, and, sure, maybe that left a wound, but my mom remarried and my stepdad, Santi, adopted me when I was a little kid and I love him like a father. I have perspective is the point. I've enjoyed advantages my entire life, and I'm smart enough to recognize how lucky I am.

How lucky I was.

I'm conscious of the drone of the funeral service around me, of the thick lump clogging my throat, the constricting itch of my jet-black pantyhose, the press of fellow mourners around me. Yet I'm also completely isolated, floating above my husband's funeral as if suspended in a bubble, watching, observing.

I'm seated in the front row, of course. The place of "honor." On my right is Justin's brittle bird of a mother, Carol. On my left is Bella, my oldest friend. She wraps a gentle arm around my shoulders, as if she senses me floating away and is trying to tether me to earth.

To Bella's left are Jahnvi and Sunil; Sunil worked with Justin and the four of us went out together many times. Jahnvi has been particularly kind during this nightmare, parking her kids at her mother's and coming by to make sure I've eaten (usually I haven't) and to see that I've "rested" (not for days).

In fact, every single employee from Justin's company, Convincer Media, is here, and they're all genuinely wrecked. Justin was their beloved leader, and they were following him to startup glory. They idolized him, or at least the success he promised them.

The pastor asks us to rise. As I do, I catch a glimpse of Will's rigid profile at the far end of the row. I know Will must be suffering as much as I am; Justin was his best friend and his business partner, and the three of us were a little family.

What are we now, with Justin gone?

A primal longing for my mother floods me. *Mommy*. I'm a grown woman, but Justin's death has rendered me a helpless child.

She's on her way back to L.A. with my stepfather, Santiago. They were in Hong Kong the day Justin's body was found, the third stop on a luxurious four-city tour that Justin had gifted them for their twenty-fifth anniversary. The trip was a dream come true for my mom, and I was as delighted as she was when Justin surprised them. The vacation was so *specific* to Mom, who had always dreamed of going to Asia. It was so extravagant, so thoughtful. So very Justin.

One travel snafu after another has left them stranded in Dallas, with no chance of getting here before tomorrow. Another reason I have to hold it together. I need my mom to promise that *it will all be okay.*

Even though I know that's bullshit. Nothing will be okay. Not ever again.

My husband lies stiff and dead in the mahogany coffin in front of me. The police say it was most likely an accident; that Justin was under the influence of *Valium,* of all things, when his car shot over a tight curve on Mulholland Drive and plummeted down a mountainside. The former I don't believe; the latter I know is ridiculous. Justin had vices, but Valium wasn't among them.

None of it seems quite real. *Could* he have been taking pills without me knowing? His younger brother died from an overdose and Justin was rigidly anti-drug, so if he was, he would have hidden it. Still, I can't quite see it.

Did he take the pills by mistake? If so, what did he think they were? Or did someone else drug him? Could someone have wanted to hurt Justin? But who? And why?

Or did the police just get it wrong?

Questions churn through my brain, but none of them have easy answers.

For days now, people have been commenting on my stoicism. How well I'm handling everything. As we sit through this service, however, I can tell that those selfsame people are starting to wonder. I must seem cold, emotionless. I just haven't been able to cry yet.

I'm afraid if I start I'll never stop. My heart is broken.

This, what I thought was the defining love affair of my life, has ended in devastating grief, a word which now consumes me.

grief [grēf]
> *noun*, deep mental anguish, as from bereavement
> **synonyms:** heartache, angst, pain, misery, woe

My very first love affair was with words. Their heft and power. Their origins and shaded meanings. Their ability to tell a story, promote an agenda, evoke a sentiment, capture a moment, steal a heart. I love the way even the simplest, most everyday words can have so many interpretations and associations, can be shaped by context or perspective. Writing has always been my sustenance.

I haven't written a single word since Justin died.

I pull my attention from this funeral home, from the rows of mourners and the pastor intoning a prayer, from Justin's mother weeping to my right, from my hands twisting in my black-clad lap. I sink back into the memory of the first time I met him: joyously, brilliantly, exceptionally *alive*.

Shock blurred the details of what happened after Justin introduced himself through my shattered windshield, although the story was told and honed so many times during the course of our relationship that it's now polished to a gleaming patina.

Justin called 911. Afraid to move me, he climbed into the car and sat next to me, asking questions, first about my well-being and then about myself. By the time the paramedics arrived he had me laughing, his inquiries ranging from my preferred type of soup to my favorite SpongeBob character.

When Justin asked if there was anyone I wanted him to call, I shook my head no. Why worry my mom and Santi in L.A.? Or anyone else for that matter. Everyone I might call was hours away. And I was fine, basically. Fine-ish, anyway.

He rode with me to the hospital, and told the admissions staff he was my brother so that they let him stay with me in the ER's curtained exam area. Justin kept up his cheerful patter as a nurse cleaned the bloody wound on my head, only drawing silent when the doctor came in to examine me.

In the end, it was nothing more than a mild concussion. Bruises from the restraint of the seatbelt and the airbag. Cuts on my face and head, largely superficial despite the quantity of blood. I glanced down at my blood-soaked clothes and my stomach curdled.

"Head wounds tend to bleed more than you'd expect," the doctor kindly reassured me.

I was lucky, that's what everyone said. A girl like me, I'm supposed to be lucky.

As the pastor asks us to stand, I touch two soft fingertips to the jagged scar that runs through my right eyebrow, an uneven white line that bisects my dark brow and gives me an unintentionally alternative look. It occurs to me that while I've stood and sat on command, I've not heard a word of this service.

Oh well. This is all mostly for the benefit of Justin's mother, Carol, anyway. It bears no connection to my private grief. I let her take over the planning of the service without thinking twice, relieved to let that burden go.

I was released from the hospital with instructions to take it easy. Justin took control, collecting my discharge paperwork and then sitting with me until I felt steady enough to leave. He called a cab to take us back to the scene of the accident, but my car had been towed away along with the pickup it had struck.

"All my stuff's in there," I choked out. I felt irrationally panicky about having to stay in my bloody clothes.

I let Justin bundle me into his Jeep, which was parked nearby, and drive me to his hotel. He escorted me into the hotel shop and purchased a set of clean clothes for me. Waited for me outside the ladies' room while I changed and bundled my blood-stiffened clothes into the plastic shopping bag.

I stared at my face in the bathroom mirror. Bandaged and swollen, I looked like a distorted cubist version of myself. My knees buckled and I grabbed the edge of the sink for support. I splashed cold water on my face. Smoothed my hair and dabbed at dried blood with handfuls of wet paper towels. Licked my dry lips.

This is as good as it's going to get. I took a deep breath and tottered out of the bathroom.

Justin led me into the hotel's cozy bar: roaring fireplace, welcoming couches in cracked leather, mellow golden lighting. He tucked a pillow behind my head and a soft knitted throw around my legs. He ordered a brandy for himself and a hot chocolate for me, all the while enveloping me in a soothing, charming waterfall of words.

It didn't occur to me to ask why this complete stranger was being so solicitous. I'm one of the lucky ones; I was used to the world treating me kindly. Or at least I was back then. Clearly, my luck has shifted.

He told me he was also up from L.A., where he now lived, but was originally from New York. He had been in Mammoth with friends, like me, but decided to stay an extra couple of days after they went back. I told him about Bella. He made a joke about injuring myself to make Bella feel guilty for leaving. I asked what he was going to do to make his friends feel guilty.

He looked deeply into my eyes and said he wasn't going to make them feel guilty, but he was *sure as hell* they were going to be jealous.

My face went hot. His *intensity*. I forgot I was battered and bruised. He made me feel *beautiful, special, extraordinary*.

I feel my face flush again here in the funeral parlor as I remember the moment.

Maybe that's why I can't cry, why I've stonewalled myself into denial. If I start to grieve, I will inevitably move through all of grief's agonizing stages, on through to acceptance. And I don't want to accept it. I don't want to move on.

CHAPTER TWO

WILL

Just say yes.

How many times did I hear those words from Justin's lips? He had a way of drawing you into whatever scheme he cooked up, no matter how crazy, with his unquenchable energy and infectious optimism.

Take the first time we met.

Back in graduate school after several years in the workforce, I was gobsmacked by how hard it was for me to readjust to the routine of classes and homework. Not to mention the undergrads. Some of them seemed impossibly young, which in turn made me feel ridiculously old. Tailgating and binge drinking; football games and Greek life. It hadn't been my thing even back in the day, which is why I did my undergrad at a smallish but prestigious liberal arts college in New England. Now I was at a big university surrounded by *kids*.

In addition, over the last couple of years, I'd made decent bank and I was struggling with the return to the poverty of student life, school loans, and ramen dinners.

I was impatient. Restless. A little lonely.

One Saturday, hungry and depressed by the meager contents of my refrigerator, I shoved my feet into sneakers, stuffed my books and computer into a backpack, and ventured out. My dingy little apartment had the advantage of being walking distance from the business school campus. That's why I'd taken it sight unseen, only to discover the proximity might have been its only true advantage. The apartment's walls were thin; my neighbors loud. The elevator threatened to stall so often I only took the stairs. Wafts of frying oil from the chicken place next door simultaneously made me hungry and turned my stomach.

My plan was to hit one of the food trucks that line up around the perimeter of the university and then make my way to the air-conditioned confines of the library. It was late on a gorgeous morning, edging into a hot afternoon.

As I emerged from my building, I nearly tripped on a square brown carton sitting just outside. A hand darted out of nowhere and jerked me away from the package just in the nick of time.

Primal fight or flight hormones flooded my system. I instinctively gripped my computer bag. Raised an arm. *To defend? To attack?* I wasn't sure, but I was ready.

Until I looked into the eyes of the man dragging me behind the box hedge that separated the vestibule from the tiny front yard. They glimmered with mischief and fun, not menace.

"Watch the box!" he cautioned in a delighted whisper as he pulled me down to a crouch. "Motion sensor."

"What the hell are you doing?" I managed to stutter, indignant and yet also somehow whispering in the same hushed tones the stranger had used, already drawn into his world.

"Sshhh. It'll just be a sec."

A woman in shades and a dyed blond ponytail pulled

through the back of a baseball cap strode briskly down the sidewalk. Upon seeing the package, she glanced around cautiously.

The stranger put a steadying hand on my shoulder and one finger to his lips.

The woman took one last glance over her shoulder. Unzipped her backpack and reached for the package. As soon as she lifted it . . .

BANG!

Loud as a gunshot, the sound reverberated in the warm air. The woman fell back on her ass and scrambled away, crawling to her feet and running down the street.

The stranger next to me leapt to his feet. "That'll teach you not to steal people's packages, you goddamn thief!" His peals of laughter chased her down the street.

He turned back to me with a radiant grin. "She's been stealing my shit for weeks. Other people's too. I even got her on video on my phone, but the police didn't want to hear about it, so I figured I'd teach her a lesson. That was awesome! Right? Just a little gunpowder wired to a touch-sensitive circuit trigger. I'm Justin. You're 3B, right? Also in the business school?"

He barely paused between sentences. I remember thinking that I should have found him off-putting (*just a little gunpowder!!*), but his smile and good humor were magnetic. "Yes, right, 3B. Will Barber. You?"

"I'm 2C. Where are you headed this fine day, Will Barber?"

"Food trucks and then library."

"Oh, I think we can do better than that."

"I really need to study."

"So do I. But look around. It's magnificent out. We should

embrace the day. Besides, I know where we can eat dumplings like kings for $12 each."

He laughed again, a full-throated chortle that made me want to join in. "Come on, Will Barber, just say yes."

I turn my head just in time to see Annie swivel away from me. I knew I'd felt her gaze. Carol battles another wave of sobs and grabs for Annie's hand. I feel awful for both of them. No mother should have to lose a child, the way Carol has. No woman should have to lose her husband so young, the way Annie has.

Beside me, my girlfriend, Molly, swishes her black-nylon-clad legs. I appreciate that she came with me today. We've not been in the best place lately and I wouldn't have blamed her if she'd begged off.

I indulge in a fantasy. The rear doors of this dreadful, somber room swing open. Justin waltzes down the center aisle in top hat and tails, twirling a white-tipped cane. He's not dead after all; it's just another in his series of robust practical jokes.

Justin was a man with an arsenal of mottoes. This ability to quote or coin a maxim for almost any situation was a ridiculous part of his charm. But his most frequent and heartfelt aphorism was:

Life's too short to ask permission. Better to ask forgiveness.

And everyone forgave Justin. He pushed limits all the time, his own as well as everyone else's, but no one could stay mad at him. He was so openly enthusiastic, so willing to laugh at himself and the world, so charming and interested, so voluble and quick.

The pounding headache I'd dispatched with Advil this morning begins to creep in again, surrounding my temples in a viselike grip. I dry swallow three more pills. Cough as they catch in my throat. Molly hands me her bottle of water and I nod my thanks. Take a swallow. It goes down hard, past a lump in my throat. Tears spring into my eyes.

I've cried over Justin's death. After Annie called to tell me his body had been found, after I saw photographs of his wrecked torso and face, again last night after I politely asked Molly to leave my apartment despite the hurt in her eyes.

I have no problem with crying. I don't do it often, but I'm not one of those guys who believe tears are a sign of weakness. I cried when all four of my grandparents died; I cried when a buddy of mine hung himself in college. I've cried for Justin and I know I'll cry for him again, although I'd prefer to do it alone, in private, away from pitying eyes.

It's not just that we were best friends and built a business together. We were a unit. For years he was my professional co-conspirator, my sounding board, my partner in crime. I planned his bachelor party and was best man at his wedding. The three of us were our own little gang, a fact that I know Molly resents.

Now he's dead and my life's work is at risk.

How will I ever figure out how to make sense of it all without him?

CHAPTER THREE

CAROL

As the service progresses, a rising wave of panic threatens to engulf me. When it's all over, my baby, my son, laid out in his crisp black wedding suit, will be rolled away and set aflame.

Is it too late to change my mind? Have him buried?

What difference does it make? Justin's dead. Whether his physical body is charred to ash or left to decay doesn't matter. He is gone.

My baby. My son.

My handkerchief is sodden with tears and snot. I press it against my raw, aching eyes. Push it harder against my eyeballs until they hurt, as if the pain will ease my devastation. It doesn't.

The sheer *range* of emotions I'm experiencing is overwhelming.

Grief. Rage. Regret. Shock. Terror. Anxiety. Loneliness.

A fresh bout of tears erupts from my swollen eyes. *Will I ever stop crying?*

It's not natural for a mother to outlive her son. It shocks. It destroys.

My husband, Justin's father, died when my boy was only ten years old. After that it was just the two of us against the world. Then he found Annie and our little family expanded. I'd hoped they'd have children; that I'd be a grandmother eventually, continue our fractured family line. Now I am alone, that hope demolished.

There's still Annie, of course, but what woman would stay linked to the mother of her now deceased spouse? Anyway, I've never quite been sure if Annie likes me. She behaved impeccably always, polite and considerate, but I felt it was motivated more by love of Justin and innate good manners than any true affection. I wish we were closer. We shared the most important man in both our lives; that should be a bond.

I stroke Annie's hand. I sense her instinct to pull away, but grasp her fingers tightly within my own. She's numb, poor thing. When it hits her, it will be *terrible*. She'll need me, even if she doesn't know it yet.

It's funny how cogent thoughts still churn through my brain, even as I cry, even as my insides are hollowed with loss. *Survival*. It is our most primal instinct and the ways in which we survive are sometimes surprising, even to ourselves.

I loved my boy so much, my mischievous, darling son.

The day Justin was born, it was hot and humid. The air was thick and sticky. Anyone with any sense had fled Manhattan for more hospitable locales. Our window air-conditioning unit was straining mightily. There had been a few rolling brownouts across the city already that summer, giving it a strained, apocalyptic tension.

I was ready for this baby. His nursery was prepared, decorated in shades of blue and green. Adorable tiny clothes were stacked inside the dresser with the changing-table top. Stuffed animals, Dr. Seuss books, and monogrammed hooded bath towels awaited my little miracle. Plus, I'd been roasting like a turkey for the last two months of my pregnancy, my ankles were swollen and my bladder in a state of perpetual leaky anxiety. I was more than ready.

Justin was a scheduled C-section—breech, and resistant thus far to efforts to turn him. Mike went out to hail a cab to take us to the hospital while I waited in the relative cool of the tiny vestibule of our apartment building on East 12th. I rubbed my belly.

"Hey there, little boy," I crooned. "Almost time to come say hello."

I watched as Mike hoisted my overnight bag up on his shoulder and lifted his arm to signal an approaching taxi. A wave of love for my husband coursed through me. We'd made this baby together. He'd be a wonderful dad. I knew this; it was one of the reasons I'd married him.

It was my choice to take just an epidural and stay awake during the procedure. I didn't want to miss a second of my boy's life. Still, it remains one of the more unnerving things I've seen in my life, the reflection of my C-section in the mirror above the operating table. My flayed skin, the blood, my organs, and my *baby*, emerging slick with viscous fluid, a matted crown of thick black hair on his head.

I was crying, I was laughing, and Mike was just the same. The nurses laid Justin on my chest. Our two hearts beat as one for too brief a moment. Justin was spirited away. They unplugged the mucus from his nose, wiped him clean, took some measurements, ran some tests, swaddled him in a striped blanket, and returned my love to me.

My heart was so full that day, that relatively ordinary August day. Seventeen other women gave birth on the same day in my hospital alone, no doubt millions more around the globe. But still, the birth of my baby, my son, on that ordinary day was extraordinary, a transcendent event, a true miracle. Maybe every mother feels that way.

My limbs feel leaden, my throat constricts. My mind flashes to Mike's funeral, how Justin pressed up against my side, his face solemn and terrified, how I whispered to him that I would always be there to take care of him.

With a chilling blast of anger, I recognize that nothing will ever close this chapter for me. *Nothing*. I will be torn ragged by Justin's death until the end of my own life.

Fury melts rapidly into despair. I release a small involuntary whimper as I finger the gray silk knotted around my throat.

I've entered the era of sleeves and scarves. A lonely old woman with crepey skin and no one left to love her.

I allow myself a healthy wallow in this self-pity. My son is dead; I'm at his funeral. If not now, when? Fresh hot tears sting and threaten.

And then, suddenly, the service is over. I will have to make my way to some bar Will has picked. Endure hours of murmured condolences and awkward sliding glances. As the hours grow later and liquor is consumed, I'm sure I'll also be subjected to a few stories about my son I'd probably be better off not knowing.

I fantasize briefly about ditching the reception; about just fleeing this dreadful place with its cloying scent of rotting flowers, its solemn rituals and painful piety, about running away and not ever coming back. But I squelch the impulse.

My son may be dead, my own life rendered meaningless, but I will give Justin the farewell he deserves.

CHAPTER FOUR

ANNIE

I couldn't bear to stay inside the funeral home while Justin burned. Carol did, staying behind to walk alongside the rolling casket as it slid into the oven. I had to turn away. Run away, if I'm being honest. I fled to the sun-baked parking lot and stumbled into my car.

I sit here, the windows rolled up tightly, the engine off, making no attempt to cool down the intense heat of the car. The seat leather is scalding, searing the backs of my legs; my dress sticks to my shoulder blades. Sweat rolls down my neck and between my breasts. The confining, airless heat of the car feels like the punishment I deserve for a crime I must have committed. I insisted on driving my own car today, which I admit doesn't make all that much sense. I probably shouldn't be on the roads; distracted, heartbroken, I'm a menace.

I just didn't want to be stranded or dependent on *anyone* on this particular day. I wanted to be able to bolt if necessary, even as I knew that was impossible. I'm the grieving widow, for fuck's sake. I need to stay front and center.

A sharp rap gets my attention. Will peers in at me.

I power on the car and roll down my window. Hot air puffs out and into Will's bearded face.

"Car sauna?" he asks with one cocked eyebrow. "Ready to pitch?"

A laugh of pure relief escapes me. This is a game the three of us played, coming up with ridiculous *Shark Tank* products and pitching them to one another.

I launch in, even though my words feel leaden. "The Car Sauna is the latest and the greatest in efficient weight-loss strategy. Who doesn't want to hop in their car and arrive five pounds lighter at their next party?"

Will continues the joke. "Bonus feature: The Car Sauna also steams the wrinkles out of your outfit. Arrive thin *and* freshly steamed everywhere you go!"

We smile at each other. Fall silent. I can see Molly hovering over Will's left shoulder.

"You okay?" he asks.

"You know," I reply, "not really."

"Still think the cocktail party is a good idea?" Will's face creases anxiously.

"It's what J would have wanted."

Will nods.

"Let us drive over with you," Will offers. "I'll leave my car here and get it later."

I nod, open the door, and slide out of the car, offering him the driver's seat. Molly joins him in the front.

Will is relieved, I can tell, which irritates me a little.

It's not like I'll drive my car into a brick wall or anything.

Then again, maybe I will.

I'm not sharing these darker thoughts with anyone, but perhaps Will's right to be relieved. He knows me well, maybe better than anyone else now that Justin's dead. Plus, shared shock, loss, and insecurity about the future bind us even more deeply than the easy friendship which had held the three of us in its tight net.

"JAWs." Justin made up the moniker. Justin. Annie. Will.

Justin used to say we were like sharks, "unstoppable." Even the shark in the movie gets taken down eventually, which I pointed out, but Justin grinned a reply: "Yeah but until then, an epic ride." I let it go. Why argue the point? It feels poignant and painful now. JAWs is just AWs; the epic ride is over.

The day Justin and I met, after the hot chocolate and brandy and a later meal of freshly baked bread and soup (he remembered and ordered my favorite, lentil), he paid for an extra room at his hotel so that I had help nearby if I needed it. The next day, he drove me to the tow yard to retrieve my luggage and skis from the destroyed Acura, and offered to drive me back to L.A. I accepted.

In that five-and-a-half-hour trip we covered a lot of ground. Justin talked with great affection about his mother (always a good sign in a man). He mentioned his father had died when he was young and then steered the conversation away, which I respected; people shouldn't have to share *everything*, in my opinion, at least not until they're ready.

He offhandedly referred to a pretty incredible Ivy League pedigree for both his undergraduate work and his MBA, and talked with great excitement about the VR startup he was launching with his best friend. He told me that first grad school and then work had pulled his focus the last few years; he hadn't dated much. He followed that admission with a cheeky grin that made me blush all over again.

And he was phenomenally interested in me. He wanted to

know all about me, asking a series of probing questions about everything from my upbringing to my education, to the places I'd been and the places I dreamed of visiting, to my current job and my aspirations for the future. I'd never felt so *seen* by a man.

He took me back to my duplex apartment in Los Feliz. Carted my luggage and skis upstairs. As I fumbled to get the key in the lock, I wondered what I should do. *Ask him in? Play hard to get?* He hadn't even asked for my number yet, although clearly he knew where I lived.

I pushed open the door and my cat, Cinnamon Toast, curled his fat calico body around my legs.

"Who's this?" Justin crooned, settling down into a crouch.

Oh my god, he even likes cats.

"Justin, meet Cinnamon Toast. C.T., meet Justin."

He stroked Cinnamon Toast's head briefly and then rose. "Well, Annie," he said. "I should get going. Are you going to be okay?"

"I am. Thank you so much for everything. I owe you."

"Then let me take you to dinner." He beamed at me, that infectious, open grin.

"Shouldn't I take you?" I asked.

Justin's eyes locked into mine. "Just say yes."

I swallowed. I felt like I was balancing on the brink of something. An adventure I hadn't known I was waiting for.

I nodded. "Yes."

I tipped into the abyss.

CHAPTER FIVE

WILL

As he'd promised, Justin did know a dumpling place in K-Town that was mad good and crazy cheap. For someone who'd landed in L.A. from New York fairly recently, he was amazingly plugged in. He seemed to have friends everywhere and a kind of Midas touch. If you were out with Justin, he knew the doorman by name, and the house always bought you a round or sent over a free dessert.

Designers gifted him clothes. Once, staring at the contents spilling from assorted slick shopping bags, I had to ask, "You get all this shit for free? Who do you have to fuck?"

"This is why we're homies," he replied cheerfully. "You're not afraid to call me on my shit. But here's the secret. I don't fuck anyone. I just let them think I might."

"And that works for you?"

"Apparently my tantalizing charms are effective on men and women alike." And there it was, his famous grin. "Listen, Will, you have to take this." He handed me a loaded shopping bag with the label of a trendy Dutch designer. "I picked everything out with you in mind."

I started to protest, but he insisted. He'd sized up for me; he couldn't wear the clothes anyway. I accepted, particularly relishing the soft comfort of a black cashmere sweater that I still own.

That was one difference between Justin and me. Where I resigned myself to scraping by on my loans and carefully hoarded savings, Justin was determined to live his best life no matter what. I was just lucky enough to be along for the ride.

He told me enough details of his life that I understood where his desire to live in the moment and live well came from. Dad dead when he was just ten, a younger half-brother with mental illness and addiction issues who drained money, time, and compassion from his poor beleaguered mother back on Long Island.

When his brother, Tommy, committed suicide during our first year of business school, Justin was crushed. He left school and we lost touch for years afterward. After we reconnected, our friendship grew stronger than ever, but he never wanted to talk about his brother or even mention his name.

I respected that, because despite all the shit Justin had endured, I'd never met someone so relentlessly, endlessly positive. No matter what bad hand he was dealt, he was always sure he'd win the game in the end.

It's a form of self-torture, but I can't help but wonder about his last thoughts as his car hurtled and bounced down the mountainside, as he stared death in the face. Was he terrified? Or was he convinced that Lady Luck would intervene to save him?

I hope it's the latter.

I hope he was optimistic and full of spirit until the very instant the life was crushed from his body.

CHAPTER SIX

CAROL

Survivor.

That word has come to mean so many different things. A side effect of a society infected by hyperbole, I suppose. A quick Internet search reveals how the word has become commodified. Survival status is emblazoned on everything from T-shirts to decorative pins, sashes and cards, banners and coffee mugs.

I survived Jackie's Bachelorette Weekend! I survived my trip to . . . Miami! Aruba! Cancun! I survived the Zombie Apocalypse!

As if real survival had anything to do with vacation, or drinking with the girls, or science fiction. I'm a *true* survivor, of my husband, of my beloved Justin, of so much more. This cheapening of the word distresses me. It's a lesser problem in our chaotic world, I understand that, but I can't help but flinch.

Alone in the back of the limo taking me to the reception Will planned, I struggle to prepare myself for the hours ahead. Condolences. Tears. Awkward hugs from virtual strangers. Anecdotes about my son that will both bring him closer and make him feel farther away. It ain't this survivor's first rodeo.

A long sigh escapes me and I realize I had been holding my breath. I open a bottle of water from the limo bar and gulp it down.

When did I last eat? Lunch yesterday.

It wasn't a conscious fast; I just forgot. I hope they've organized food along with the alcohol.

Air. Water. Food. I'd argue *love* is another essential tenet of survival as it creates *will,* the *will* to live, the *will* to find the strength and resilience to *keep going and do what must be done.*

My mind ticks along with these random thoughts; they form a perimeter around the chasm of my grief.

Loss is cumulative, I've come to believe. Each fresh sorrow scraping raw the tender scars of the previous ones. If I tip into the void it will swallow me whole.

When I was fifteen, the rest of my family was killed in a freak house fire. The blame was placed on shoddy electrical wiring in the newly built suburban "dream home" my parents had purchased in pursuit of their version of the American Dream.

I should have died too; I would have, if I hadn't snuck out to meet Bobby Tanaka, a year ahead of me in high school. I had my first kiss and lost both of my parents, my older sister, and my little brother all in the same night.

The fire became the single event that defined me. Life before the fire was one thing. Life after it, entirely different. The pervasive stench of tragedy followed me.

I don't talk about it much anymore, which is a relief. As it was the defining thing in my life for so many years, I was happy to let it recede. In the immediate aftermath, of course, the subject was paramount as my extended family tried to determine what to do with me. Then the story was shaped for my college essays, which netted me a full ride to NYU. Don't get me wrong, my grades and scores were good, but I know it was my special tragedy that bought me my slot, that made me *special*.

Once I was finally at school, almost every new encounter stalled when we got to the inevitable subjects of siblings, parents' occupations, or holiday plans. It got so I could predict the reactions. Shocked dismay led to either awkward silence or a rush of over-compensatory effulgence along the lines of *"Come to my house for Thanksgiving! I'm sure my parents would love to have you!"*

I usually accepted these invitations. I wanted those windows into other homes and families. I relished the treatment I received from my friends' mothers in particular. The poor orphan girl brought about an onrush of maternal coddling. I was told to sleep in, wasn't allowed to help with the dishes, and was treated to little gifts. These excursions were far superior to returning to my aunt and uncle for holidays, with their sour marriage and three screaming little boys.

It was also on one of these family visits that I met Mike. I was a junior in college, returning to my friend Robyn's home in Vermont for the second Christmas in a row. Last year, it had just been Robyn and her parents, and they had treated us like princesses. Favorite snacks laid in, piles of presents for us both, lavish dinners out.

This year Robyn's older brother was also coming. Robyn was indifferent. She thought her big brother was weird. For me, it was love at first sight.

Up until the day Mike died, we lived a valentine. He *was* a little weird, but a sweetheart, a gangly, crooked-toothed, shaggy-haired shambles of a man, with a fierce heart and a fast mind. He gave me a kind of stability I hadn't had before and haven't had since.

Justin occasionally admonished me for idealizing his dad, his brow furrowing in irritation. He argued that Mike couldn't have been that perfect; no one was. Wasn't it better to love and mourn the real man rather than a fiction?

I chalked it up to a kind of jealousy. After all, Justin was a little boy when his father died; he and I shared the closeness many single moms develop with their sons. How many times did people tell him he was now "the man of the house"? How could he *not* want to be primary in my affection?

The day Justin took on the mantle of "man of the house" began like most. We were living on Long Island then; Mike left early to drive to his job in the city. I dropped Justin at school and went to the local real estate office where I was a broker. We had a team meeting and then I had three showings, a busy day. Justin had Robotics Club after school.

I was at my last showing of the day. The Kleins and I stepped out onto the porch of the house I had just shown them. They agreed to make an offer and I was ecstatic; I'd been carrying the listing for months. A police patrol car pulled up in front. As soon as the cops got out of their cruiser, I knew something was wrong. Terribly wrong.

A five-car pileup on the Long Island Expressway had claimed three lives. There had been a fire, so they'd only just been able to positively identify Mike. He'd been dead since 8:11 that morning. Over seven hours had passed.

How had I not known? How had his soul left this earth without me feeling it?

Fire. He died in a fire.

Later I was told I had fainted, that if Marty Klein, former

high school quarterback, hadn't been so quick, I would have crashed right onto the brick porch.

When I awoke, I was in a hospital bed. Justin was the first thing I saw, perched on an orange plastic guest chair, fists bouncing on his knees, his bright eyes searching mine.

"Mom! You're up!"

One of the cops who had broken the news moved into my line of sight. "How are you feeling, Carol?" he asked. "You fainted on us there. Gave us quite a scare."

I pushed up to a sitting position and opened my arms for my son. Justin crawled in. I addressed the cop over his head, "Does he know?"

"No, ma'am," he answered softly. "We thought that should be up to you."

And then I had to tell my little boy that his father was dead. *Survive that, bitches.*

CHAPTER SEVEN

ANNIE

The blare of a car horn makes me jump. I flick my eyes forward. The light is green. We're not moving. Will jerks my car into the intersection. *Maybe he shouldn't be driving either.*

Rigid beside Will in the front of the car, Molly desperately tries to read him. I can see it in her anxious, sidelong glances and tense jaw. If we were friends I would tell her that the best thing she could do right now is back off, give Will some space. But we're not friends really, Molly and I, and I have my own troubles.

Maybe Molly wasn't all that wrong when she complained about being unable to break into JAWs' inner ring. She's *fine*, but she isn't one of us.

I should be more charitable, shouldn't I? Kinder? It's hard to muster when I feel so eviscerated. I chide myself: *Do better, be better.*

Oh fuck it. Not today.

From our first encounter on, Justin promised me a life full of surprises. He was exuberant, generous, sensitive, expansive, a little bit mad. He brought me out of my shell, even as I found myself holding my breath wondering how far he would go.

For our first real date, Justin planned a day of gallery hopping in downtown L.A., with lunch at a charming Vietnamese restaurant still in its soft open. It went on to become one of the hottest spots in the city. I learned that he was always the first one in the know, tipped off about the hot new restaurant, the up-and-coming band, the edgiest new street artist or fashion label. He seemed to know endless people, all interesting, all interested in him, and by extension me. He was more inside L.A. than I, a lifelong resident, was. He made me feel glamorous.

We ended our first date at a trendy millinery shop owned by a friend of his, where he picked out a hat for me. It was a natural straw number with a navy and white silk striped band, and maybe the only hat that ever looked good on me. Justin kissed me for the first time after he paid for it, ducking his head under the shallow brim for a quick soft kiss on my parted lips that sent an electric shock through my system.

Our first few weeks together zipped along at a giddy pace. Justin wooed me in an old-fashioned way: flowers, dinners at trendy restaurants, thoughtful little gifts (the aforementioned straw hat, a stainless steel bracelet engraved with the longitude and latitude for Mammoth Mountain, a LACMA umbrella in the midst of a particularly rainy week). These presents were perfect: personal, considerate, and appropriately modest for a relationship in the early stages.

I felt deeply cared for, and also acutely longed for, as Justin kept his desire known but our physical contact restricted to kisses and nuzzles. This lasted for *weeks*. At first he claimed consideration for the injuries I'd sustained in the car accident. And in truth, with my busted-up nose and split lip, swollen eyes and sore jaw, I was grateful.

The delayed physical intimacy also gave us a chance to build a relationship on the basis of shared conversation and confidences. I discovered Justin really cared about how I saw my life unfolding (unlike most men I'd dated, or even just met, for that matter). I work in PR; it pays the bills. But I dream of supporting myself as a fiction writer, an admission I rarely made in those days.

A slew of brutal rejections of my first post-graduation submissions had made me gun-shy. A few years later, I tried again, only to get *no response at all* to at least 75 percent of my attempts. Was my work so dreadful that people couldn't even be bothered to *reply*? I felt smaller than a pebble. I packed up my dream of a literary career and tucked it away. I committed to being the best damn PR rep for MediFutur that I could be.

And I was good. Am good. It's surprising how complicated public relations can be for a medical technology company. My work is both industry- and public-facing. The company is on the cutting edge of some technologies that are going to be literally life-changing and lifesaving. I take pride in working there. Or rather did take pride in working there. I can't imagine walking back into the place now.

I force my attention back to my early days with Justin, a much more pleasant place for my thoughts to linger.

A turning point in our already fevered relationship came about when Justin asked to read some of my writing. I emailed him three of my favorite short stories. I was terribly nervous. I even sent him a text telling him to delete them without reading them. What if he rejected them like everyone else? *What if he rejected me?*

I didn't hear from him for three days. I was manic with worry. I was convinced that not only did he hate my work, but that he hated it so much that he was going to break up with me. How could Justin Childs, charismatic, enigmatic, connected, and charming, stand to be with me, an abject failure at my chosen craft?

failure [ˈfāl-yər]
> *noun,* 1. the condition or fact of not achieving the desired end or ends; 2. one that fails; 3. the condition of being insufficient or falling short
> **synonyms:** incompetent, bankrupt, non-performer, underachiever, loser, flunker, turkey, flop, has-been, no-account, dud, derelict, dead duck

That was the drumbeat in my head.

When Justin texted to confirm our dinner plans for Friday, I was relieved. Still, I continued to torture myself, imagining that he was merely doing me the courtesy of breaking up in person.

I made certain to look *killer* for our date. It was like pulling on a suit of armor. I turned heads walking in to meet him at the restaurant, which Justin clearly clocked. He greeted me with a kiss and a possessive embrace. Then he launched into his *delight* about my stories. He discussed them with me intelligently, his eyes lighting up with questions and ideas. I was relieved. No, more than that. I was ecstatic.

A week later, he gave me a leather journal embossed with the letter *A,* and a gold pen with exquisite heft and flow. On the first page, he inscribed,

To Annie, Never Stop
Love, J

He made me believe in myself as a writer again. This, of all Justin's many gifts to me over the course of our time together, was the one for which there was not then, and now will never be, an adequate thank-you.

As time went on, I healed and we heated. I wanted more than chaste kisses, but it was Justin who pulled back. He cupped my tender jaw between his two warm palms. "Annie, something unusual is going on here. Would you agree?"

Mesmerized by the sweet brightness in his eyes, I could only manage a nod.

"I have a feeling we'll have our whole lives to go to bed together. So let's wait a little. Keep us both in suspense?"

How sexy was that? He sealed the question with the lightest of kisses. It made me crazy with desire for him.

Needless to say, when we finally did take each other to bed, it was explosive. Sex added a delicious layer to a relationship that was already forged in intellectual connection, similar senses of humor, and like wells of hopeful ambition.

We began to merge and enmesh. We left toothbrushes at each other's places. I wore his hoodies. He wrapped a scarf of mine around his neck and claimed it as his. I feigned outrage and he sugared the theft with a wink and the assurance that it was only so he could inhale my scent when we were apart.

How am I going to survive the next few hours? How will I survive the rest of my life?

Will and Molly are looking at me, I realize. I've stopped short in front of the entrance to the Pickford, the location of Justin's funeral reception. I was so deep in my own thoughts

I'm shocked to find myself here. I don't remember Will parking, or getting out of the car, or walking over to the entrance.

"I've got you," Will says kindly. He tucks his arm through mine and draws me into the cool, dark interior of the pub. Molly trails after us.

A spotlight shines on a photograph of Justin on an easel. As my eyes connect with the eyes in the image, a shiver courses through my body. For a moment, it was like looking right into Justin's beautiful *living* face. A sharp, angry slice of regret and loss pierces my gut.

I still can't believe he's gone. Maybe none of this is really happening?

Will guides me to a table. I find a glass of whiskey in my hand. I lift the glass to Justin's photograph in a toast. Take a sip. Feel a single tear slip from the side of my right eye.

Is this the beginning of the end? Will the tears start now and never stop?

Will places a box of tissues and a plate loaded with cheese, crackers, olives, and carrots on the table in front of me. Molly follows with a glass of water. "You should eat something, Annie," Will admonishes me. "Don't want to drink on an empty stomach." He puts one of his large square hands on my shoulder and I feel instantly comforted.

When I first met Justin, he told me there were two essential people in his life, his business partner, Will, and his mother, Carol.

He described Will as his best friend and "the brother I hadn't known I was missing, until he was found."

He said Carol was "the person who taught me everything I know about love."

I met Will first, which was only natural. We all lived in L.A., while Carol was still living on the East Coast back then. Justin and I had been dating just a few weeks, six maybe, when he casually suggested Will join us for dinner, *that very night.*

Justin had built a mythology around his friend Will, so much so that he loomed larger than life. Will had *saved Justin's life* their first year of B school. Will knew Justin better than anyone. Will had sacrificed his steady job and staked his savings to partner with Justin in their startup VR venture, Convincer Media. Will was Justin's *hero.*

Talk about pressure.

I must have changed outfits a dozen times before I finally settled on jeans, boots, and a featherweight cashmere sweater in a flattering shade of coral. Casual but put together, attractive but not flaunting it. I wanted to make the right impression, whatever that meant. I just knew I desperately wanted Will to like me.

That night was so like Justin. He picked me up, that glint of mischief in his eyes. Told me not to ask questions.

We met Will at the OUE Skyspace LA, and though it's a popular tourist destination now, somehow Justin got the three of us in for a private tour before the place's official opening. Located on the sixty-ninth floor of an office building downtown, the exhibit is a loving ode to Los Angeles. Soon we were darting around the interactive exhibits: at the shadow wall watching our mirrored reflections dissolve into particles, circling the 360-degree panoramic view of the city, staring down into the infinity mirror, which creates the illusion of staring straight down to the very bottom of the skyscraper.

Justin saved the "best" for last, a ride down the Skyslide, a forty-five-foot glass-enclosed tube that carries brave souls from the seventieth floor down to the sixty-ninth on the *outside of the building.*

Talk about pressure.

I was terrified, but Justin and Will were *ebullient,* high-fiving, jostling each other to see who would go first. It was Justin in the end, no surprise.

Will and I watched him take off down the slide with a mighty *whoop!*

"Do you want to go next?" Will asked. Our eyes met and his softened. "You don't have to do it if you don't want to."

He was trying to be kind, but I bristled. He and Justin were a club and I wanted in.

"I'll go," I answered, struggling to control the waver in my voice.

"He has that effect, doesn't he?" Will said gently.

"What do you mean?"

"Justin. He gets people to push their boundaries. He sure as hell gets me to push mine." Will gifted me a warm smile. "Hasn't killed me yet."

Unsure how to reply, I entered the slide. Squeezed my eyes shut and didn't open them once on the way down. Fell into a pair of familiar arms. Peeled my eyelids open. Justin gazed at me in a way that made me squirm with desire, to kiss him, to fuck him, to please him, to *enchant* him.

"Wasn't that incredible?" His eyes shone. He rocked back and forth on his heels as if gravity was struggling to contain him.

Will whooshed down into the soft landing pit. "Woot! Woot! Woot!" he shouted. "Amazing! Fucking amazing!"

Lit up with adrenaline and adventure, we went on to drinks

and dinner and more drinks. Near the close of the night, Justin christened us "JAWs." After we shut our last bar down, the three of us roamed the streets humming the iconic shark theme from the movie, arms linked, with me in the middle.

We felt invincible. Or at least I did.

CHAPTER EIGHT

WILL

A car horn startles me. I was so lost in thought, I was completely unaware of the traffic. I lift my foot off the brake and accelerate as a metallic tang fills my mouth. I've worried at my inner bottom lip with my teeth until I've drawn blood.

I was seven the first time I did that, gnawed at my lip until it bled. Cowering under my covers in my bedroom upstairs while my parents raged in the kitchen below, the rise and fall of anger and recrimination that I couldn't quite decipher, punctuated by the sounds of crashes, thuds, and shattering glass.

Ours was not a violent household. My father is an anthropology professor at Stanford (his specialty, the study of tools and their effect on society); my mother is a clinical psychologist. Palo Alto is a wealthy liberal enclave; we had *family councils* about *how I might have disappointed*, but I was rarely punished, *never* struck.

Alarmed by my own bloody mouth, afraid to know what was happening and yet desperately needing to see, I chose to brave the sounds of violence below. I crept out of my bedroom and down the stairs.

Just in time to see Daddy punch Mommy in the eye.

I don't remember how I got there, but suddenly I was cling-ing to my father's back, dribbling blood on his white collar, shrieking, "Stop it! Stop it! Stop it!"

I rained my small fists on my father's broad shoulders. He paused in his advance on my mother. Dropped his raised arm. My mother reached out to me and I leapt to her. We sank to the floor wrapped in each other. Through my tears, I caught the glinting wreckage of broken glass strewn across the floor.

My father squared his slumped shoulders, went to the pan-try, and pulled out a broom. Meticulously swept up the shards of glass without saying a single word. Mom lifted me onto the kitchen counter and put paper-towel-wrapped ice on my bloody lip. Asked me to hold it there while she wetted down yet more paper towels and swabbed the kitchen floor for the finest par-ticles of glass. Then she picked me up and carried me back upstairs and tucked me into bed, sitting with me until I dropped off to sleep.

The next morning it was as if the whole incident had been a nightmare, something I'd conjured, not quite real. My parents circled me and my little brother, Chris, barely two years old and plunked into his high chair, with their usual practiced rou-tine. Coffee for them. Breakfast for us. Confirmation that Mom would pick up Chris at daycare; that Dad would get me after basketball practice.

After Dad grabbed his briefcase and darted out for his first class, I studied my mother's face. She'd covered it with makeup, but there was a reddish bruise on the bloom of her cheek.

"I don't want Daddy to get me after practice," I announced.

Mom sighed. "He loves you very much, Will." Her eyes were

wet with tears, which surprised and alarmed me. "I promise you that. You are his everything."

Dad did pick me up after practice, and though I was initially wary of him, he seemed to be the Dad I knew, affable, a little distracted, kind, not the monster I'd glimpsed the night before. He took me out for burgers, just the two of us.

I was prepared for the worst; Allison Greenspan, a girl in my class, had recently announced at recess that her parents were getting a divorce. Allison had been delighted by the prospect, two houses, two sets of toys, two closets full of dresses, and *no more fighting*. I was more ambivalent.

But as we shared fries and sipped milkshakes, Dad surprised me. "Will, I want you to know how very sorry I am," he launched in. "About what you saw last night, that you saw it, that it happened at all. I've apologized to your mother and I'm apologizing to you."

I'd been forced to apologize by my parents on multiple occasions, to them and to others; this was the first time I could remember my father apologizing to me.

The salty potato in my mouth suddenly felt like it was choking me. I'd almost convinced myself that last night had been a dream. But no, it was real. And now Dad was apologizing?

"People lose their tempers sometimes. It's not admirable, but it happens. I lost mine. I won't try to rationalize it or justify it. But as you've gone seven years, five months, and four days without seeing me lose it like I did last night, I'll do my best to make sure it takes at least another eight or so years until you see me like that again. Deal?" He smiled his same old Dad smile at me.

I took a sip of cold vanilla shake and dislodged the fry in my throat.

"Deal."

Things went back to normal after that. We did our usual family things: We had our early Sunday dinners with the same faculty clique of parents with similarly aged children. Dad and I worked on projects together, from restoring an old car to building a coffee table. He taught me about his love of tools and the value of respecting them (the reason I always have a toolbox in my trunk). He took me to my first concerts and instilled his love of '60s rock in me. He came to my games and cheered from the sidelines. Mom ferried Chris and me to the library, to the park, to playdates and practices.

Yet nothing was the same. In ways I could never quite put my finger on.

When Chris finally went off to college, six years after I'd done the same, my parents split up. The next summer when I was home for a visit, my mother announced over vodka tonics that Chris and I had different biological fathers, his being a former student of my dad's with whom she'd had an affair.

My world spun on its axis. "Does Chris know?"

"Yes."

"Does Dad know?"

"Yes."

"How long have they known?"

"Chris I told the summer before he went away to school. As for your dad, you probably don't remember, Will," my mother replied. "But you might. You were seven or eight? Chris was still a toddler."

Her eyes met mine and I knew exactly which night it had been when Dad learned the truth.

"And he stayed with you? All that time?" Hurt and anger I hadn't begun to process made my words harsh.

Mom flinched, just a little. "We loved each other and we loved you boys. We decided we would work it out."

"Until you didn't," I spat out bitterly.

"That's fair," Mom said. "But life is long and complicated, Will. You can live many lives in the course of one."

I was angry at her for a long time. And at my dad too. That relationship never really recovered (particularly after he got remarried to a student named *Brandy* and had baby twin girls that he announced with oblivious joy were his chance to do fatherhood *right*).

I distanced myself from Chris, the tangible proof of my mother's infidelity. I learned that no one can be wholly trusted.

Thinking about trust makes me wonder about Warren Sax, Justin's mentor and our company's biggest investor. I haven't heard a word from Sax since Justin died, despite leaving phone messages and sending an email to the private address I found on Justin's computer. I thought he would turn up for the funeral, but I haven't spotted him.

Sax is notoriously reclusive. And while I loved Justin, he was admittedly a bit of a narcissist. I recognize that was part of the reason he kept Sax in such a silo. Justin alone could charm the legend, that was made clear.

Justin kept his line of communication with Sax so personal and direct that I've never even met the guy. I can't help but wonder if he'll continue to back us with Justin gone. My stomach knots.

Yet another fucking unknown. Questions have been throbbing in my head, a relentless drumbeat:

How and why did Justin go over that embankment? Accident? Suicide? *Murder?*

The Valium found in his system makes me wonder. He hated drugs. Never used them.

Did someone kill Justin? And if so, who? *Why?*

I pull into a parking space next to the bar I selected for the reception. I watch as black-clad mourners make for the entrance; I know most of them. It seems absurd, it seems insane, but I have to ask myself: Could one of them be Justin's killer?

CHAPTER NINE

CAROL

A peal of laughter floats over the buzz of the crowd. I recognize the laugh; it's Annie's, a hearty bellow right from the gut. I don't begrudge her; I'm glad. She'll have enough tears later.

I flash to Mike's funeral. Shards of memory pierce me like daggers: Justin clinging to my side, mute. Mike's parents, as shell-shocked as I was. His sister, Robyn, tending to all of us. The fight that ensued when I walked in on her grinding a pill and snorting it in Justin's bedroom after the service.

"Everyone deals with grief differently," Robyn defiantly shouted when I challenged her.

She was right, of course, but she also died of an overdose four years later.

This bar Will picked is packed with hipsters. These kids all think they're so unique and quirky, but they fall into obvious stereotypes. Tattoos, piercings, and leather are one set of signifiers. Then there are the proud nerds with their square glasses and jaunty hats, 1950s dresses and dainty handbags. The techies are identified by their streamlined silhouettes and sleek, futuristic fabrics.

I wonder if anything or anyone has the ability to surprise me anymore.

That sweet girl Molly brings me over a plate of food. She's besotted with Will, that much is obvious. Poor thing. Men will break your heart one way or another.

After Mike died, I was our sole support. I got an insurance settlement in connection with his accident, but I put it in trust for Justin's college education. We had to sell our home and move to a townhouse in a less desirable neighborhood. My boy and I leaned heavily on each other, isolated in a shared bitter grief.

I did the best I could. That's all one can ask of any mother, right? I loved my son; I kept a roof over his head and food in his belly. I sacrificed most of my own small pleasures for his greater good and never regretted it. I had lost my parents, my sister, and my brother. I had lost Mike. Justin was my life raft.

Then Robyn died, and her parents followed shortly thereafter. Brokenhearted by the loss of both their children, they simply seemed to lose the will to live.

Justin was all I had. I was all he had.

I began to dream about my sister and brother. Each night as I slept, they rose up from a pile of burnt ash to circle me, locked forever at the ages at which they died, seventeen and eleven respectively.

My parents didn't haunt me this way, and hard as I prayed, I couldn't conjure Mike in my dreams either. Maybe it was for the best. I imagined seeing him would bring me solace, but my siblings' visitations only brought a panicked fear.

Justin started getting into trouble at school. I didn't blame him, I felt like picking fights all the time myself. But the third time I was pulled away from a house showing by a call from the school office, I was beside myself.

When I strode into the principal's office, Justin was perched on a chair, an ice pack applied to his bloody nose. Our eyes met and he must have seen some of the steel in mine because he cowered.

I covered his ass with the principal, asking for time and promising counseling, playing the poor-widowed-woman-and-bereft-son card as hard as I could. It was true, after all, even if I was frustrated with Justin. And I was even more frustrated with myself. I couldn't help him. I didn't know how. I didn't know how to help myself.

We walked in silence to the school parking lot. Climbed into my Volvo wagon. Sat in silence for what felt like an eternity.

Finally, I began. "Look, honey, I know this is a tough time. But I promise you that getting into fights is pretty much guaranteed *not* to make it any better. You're angry. I understand that. I am too. But we need to figure out how to manage that anger, not turn it on other people. Or ourselves."

I could see a pulse beat in his temple, even as he kept his gaze fixed out the front windshield.

"Justin? Do you understand me?" Exasperation wrenched my voice. "I can't keep just abandoning clients! If I don't sell houses, we don't eat."

True fear drove my words. The membrane that kept us from tipping off the grid into despair and homelessness felt very thin.

I could see that the harshness of my tone scared him, but I couldn't stop. "You can't do this anymore! Do you understand? I have enough on my plate! I can't take on this fighting bullshit too!"

I regretted the words as soon as they left my mouth. The last thing I wanted to do was pass my worries on to Justin. It was my job to reassure him the world was safe, despite evidence to the contrary.

He stayed turned away from me. The idea of a division between the two of us was sickening. But I had to get through to him. I grabbed his arm. "Do you understand, Justin? Just say yes."

Justin turned his troubled eyes to mine. "Yes," he said so softly I could barely hear him.

We stayed there in the car in silence for a few moments longer. I felt deflated. Upset with myself for losing my temper. Uncertain about how to make it better. Afraid that one false move could send our fragile existence toppling.

We went out for pizza, got through homework and the rest of the nightly routine.

Later that night, I stood in the shadowy doorway of his room and stared at Justin as he slept, my darling boy, his face damaged by fists he'd sought. I cried.

As the days and weeks went on, I worried, of course, but Justin never got in another fight. It became a joke between us, "Just say yes!" when either of us wanted the other to do something.

It strikes me suddenly that I'm no longer tied to California. I moved out here to be close to Justin and Annie, with the hope of grandchildren down the line. This realization is freeing, and at the same time, frightening. Nothing and no one links me anywhere anymore.

I scan the room for Annie. Will is whispering something in her ear. I wouldn't be surprised if the two of them got together after an "appropriate" period of time. My eyes narrow as Annie puts a hand on his shoulder. *Are they together already?*

My sadness turns to a hard knot of rage. How dare they be alive when Justin is dead? How dare they think of a future beyond him? I realize my fists are clenched; my shoulders hunched almost to my ears.

I roll my shoulders to release some of the tension. I know I'm being unkind. It's just that I so desperately need to find some reason for my staggering loss that their very existence feels like an affront.

CHAPTER TEN

ANNIE

I step away from Will and feel my legs wobble. I must have had at least three whiskeys. My cousin Lizzie, inky black hair pulled in a bun so high and tight it gives me a headache just looking at it, comes over and grips my forearms.

"Anything you need!" she slurs at me. (*I'm not the only one who's been drinking.*) "I mean it, Annie, you need anything at all, you just call me! Aunt Laura and Uncle Santiago are still delayed? Terrible!"

Lizzie always makes me feel a little *less than;* not entirely her fault really, she's just always so polished and perfect. She's a high-level Hollywood publicist who frequently boasts she can get to anyone in the world in three phone calls. I don't think she means to be smug, necessarily, but who feels the need to assert that claim repeatedly?

Lizzie sways into me. Her breath is hot, both sweet and sour. "I will do anything you need, Annie," Lizzie reassures earnestly. "I can reach anyone in the world in three phone calls you know, so just speak up!"

Predictable.

I turn my head away and see Carol staring from across the bar. She looks small and forlorn, a bit at sea among the crowd of mourners.

When Justin told me he wanted me to meet his mother, my heart skipped a beat. I knew how close they were and how much her approval would matter if Justin and I were to progress to the next step.

Justin suggested we take advantage of the upcoming Memorial Day weekend and extend for a few days beyond. He and Will were riding high with the company and Justin was confident leaving the helm for a little while. He planned a packed itinerary of dinners, theater outings, and sightseeing for the three of us.

Once we were settled in for the flight from L.A. to New York, Justin took my hand and graced me with one of his magnificent smiles. "Excited?"

"More like nervous," I replied.

"No need to be. She's going to love you." He gave my hand a squeeze.

Once we'd taken off, Justin promptly went to sleep. I tried to nap as well, but I was buzzing with excitement and nerves. This was my first visit to New York City. I was in love. I was meeting the mother of the man I hoped to marry.

I felt like I was on the precipice of *my life*. It was a little crazy; clearly I had a life before I met Justin. But with him as my partner I felt bold and brave and *special*. I truly believed that the two of us together could do anything. This visit had to be perfect.

Talk about pressure.

She was waiting for us as soon as we entered baggage claim at JFK. Small in stature, gigantic in energy, Carol hurled herself at Justin and wrapped her arms around his neck. He bent forward to embrace her in return, shooting a sweet, shy smile at me over her head. I fell in love just a little bit deeper then. That glance told me he wasn't afraid to let me see his vulnerabilities and that his deep connection with his mother was one of them.

After they unhinged, Carol pivoted toward me with arms outstretched. "Annie!" she exclaimed. "I feel like I know you already!" She enfolded me in a hug that was too long and too tight. My neck craned uncomfortably. When I tried to pull away, she only drew me closer.

"Come on, Mom, let the woman breathe." Justin laughed.

Despite her warm welcome, and how delighted Carol appeared to be with every extravagant plan Justin triumphantly presented, I never quite found a rhythm with her that trip. There was nothing overt, she wasn't ever rude or even cool to me, but rather unfailingly kind, inclusive, and perpetually chatty. I put it down to the normal protectiveness any mother would have about a son's new girlfriend, magnified by the especially close bond these two shared.

And anyway, Justin seemed oblivious to any tension, real or imagined. He kept telling us both how wonderful it was to have his "two best girls together at last." He shared his attention between us in such a way that I always felt he was taking care of me, even when he was tending to Carol. On our last night, in a taxi on the way to meet his mother for dinner, Justin pronounced the trip a huge success.

"She loves you as much as I do," he asserted.

That night we dined at one of New York's iconic restaurants, the old-fashioned Gramercy Tavern. Justin ordered champagne. We all got a little giddy. I finally felt a bit looser around Carol. I saw the way she looked at Justin and I was certain my gaze when contemplating him must be much the same. We both loved him, that should be enough to connect us, right?

I tottered off to the restroom between our salads and our entrées. The fizz of the champagne stoked my anticipation; I began to suspect that tonight was *the night*. I patted some cold water on my face and squared off against my reflection in the mirror. "Mrs. Justin Childs," I whispered. "Annie Childs."

My lips twisted wryly. I'd never said those words out loud before. "Annie Childs" didn't have the ring I'd expected. "Annie Elizabeth Childs," I whispered at my reflection. *Better.* "Annie Hendrix Childs." *Good too.*

It may sound retro to some, how eager I was to give up my own name or at least add Justin's to it. I have my father's last name; how is that any less patriarchal? Besides, I knew I would feel nothing but pride being Justin's wife; I felt that every day as his girlfriend. Why wouldn't I want to announce my partnership with him to the world?

Carol and Justin didn't see me at first when I returned from the restroom. His head was bowed to hers, her lips moving furiously, her small hand gripped tightly around his wrist. This was a side of her I hadn't seen during the course of this visit. The intensity, much like Justin's. The ferociousness, all her own. She looked like she was lecturing him or warning him about something, although I was too far away to hear a word.

Was she warning him away from me?

Drawing to the side for a moment, I kept watch as Justin nodded somberly. Then he reached out and stroked his mother's hair in a comforting gesture. The intimacy of the exchange made me squirm for some reason.

Don't be silly, I chastised myself. *Too much champagne, too little solid food.*

I hustled back to our table and was seated just in time for our main courses. The arrival of the food, the offers of freshly ground pepper and another bottle of bubbly occupied all of our attention. The food was delicious; we all shared bites. Dessert was out of this world—a tower of chocolate in myriad formats: creams, mousses, bars, cakes, crumbles, cookies.

With a good-natured giggle, Carol complained about how fat she'd gotten during the course of our visit. I was happy to tell her quite sincerely that she was speaking nonsense; she was gorgeous. She reached one hand to me and one to Justin.

"Thank you for coming, children."

"Our pleasure, Mom," Justin replied, beaming at us both.

We sat there just a moment longer, Carol in the middle, companionably enveloped by the decadent comfort of an expensive and delicious meal. I decided I had misread the intensity of the moment I'd observed. She'd been nothing but lovely this whole visit.

Excusing myself to Lizzie, I head in Carol's direction. After all, the two of us are the most broken by Justin's death; there's a grotesque comfort in that. She pulls a plastic vial from her handbag and pops a pill, tucking the container back away as I approach.

"Will did a nice job," I offer, gesturing to the packed bar. Indeed, a merry group surrounds us, drinking and laughing and talking. A handful of people are gathered around the journal Will provided for reminiscences. There will be an opportunity for short speeches and then a buffet dinner of hamburgers,

French fries, grilled cheese, and spaghetti and meatballs: comfort foods. Music and dancing to follow. It's just what Justin would have wanted.

"Yes," Carol says. She grips my hand tightly in hers, so fiercely it hurts. I struggle against my impulse to wrench it away. "You'll get through this," she hisses at me, only making me more uncomfortable.

I tug my hand free and enfold the smaller woman in an embrace as a way of avoiding the intensity of her gaze. She feels brittle, her bones as light as a bird's. "You will too," I reassure kindly.

I feel a poignant sense of wonder about my mother-in-law. Having lost her nuclear family, her husband, and now both of her sons, how is she still even upright?

For that matter, is she still my mother-in-law? I don't have a road map for this.

With a rush of empathy, I blurt out, "I can't imagine the losses you've experienced, Carol. You're really an inspiration. First your family when you were just a kid, then your husband, then Tommy, now Justin . . ." A sob catches in my throat and she pulls her body away from my embrace.

"Tommy?" she asks with an odd glint in her eye.

"I'm sorry," I stutter, suddenly remembering that Justin hated talking about his brother who died, and had warned me multiple times his mother could barely stand to hear the sound of his name. Carol never spoke about her younger son. *Fuck.* "Never mind, I don't know what I'm saying. Let's get you a drink, I can't believe you're empty-handed."

I steer Carol over to the bar and procure a glass of white wine for her. When a friend from work comes to offer condolences, I'm grateful for the opportunity to turn away and then drift deeper into the crowd. As I accept hugs and tears and promises of *dinners soon,* a chill burrows deep into my heart and soul.

If Carol could deny the existence of one son, would she deny the existence of the other? Would Justin also become too difficult to talk about and so never mentioned or named? Would that happen to me? Would I start to avoid mentioning Justin until he was *erased*?

The whiskey in my stomach sours.

CHAPTER ELEVEN

WILL

When Justin left L.A. and went back to New York just before our finals because of his brother's death, he assured me he'd be back the next semester. He didn't show.

I reached out to him several times, but he didn't reply. I was sucked into the grind of studying, and the circle of people around me.

I graduated. Took a job with a company specializing in tech development investments. I was making bank again and enjoying life, but living modestly. I had a plan. I was gathering experience and laying a financial safety net. I knew eventually I wanted to be my own man, have my own company, and my antennae were up for the next opportunity.

When April Riley, our receptionist, knocked on the glass door of the conference room one sunny afternoon, it was clear she was in the grip of *something*. A high flush colored her cheeks; a bounce marked her steps. She opened the door and a *giggle* floated into the space.

The five of us in the room turned as one and looked at her expectantly. Our office was open plan; if we were sequestered in the one glass booth we had, there was a reason. We all had cellphones. There was a landline on the conference room table. Why was April in here *giggling*?

"Will," she managed. "I was asked to deliver a message in person. '*Just say yes*.'" With that, April blushed.

Justin Childs was waiting in reception, back from the dead.

"Brother!" he cried upon seeing me. "I owe you a massive apology."

Apologize he did. And explain, over a long evening that involved many martinis, blood-red steaks, and after dinner brandies.

Justin had gone home after his brother's suicide to discover his mother's affairs were in worse shape than he had realized. His brother had duped her into signing over power of attorney and had burned through most of her savings before he died. He'd even taken out a second mortgage on her home. There was no way Justin could leave her alone and come back to L.A.

I understood. I thought it was selfless and brave and I told him so. But I also asked why he had disappeared on me.

Justin dropped his head into his palm. "Yeah, that's really on me, man. Truth? After . . . after I left, I was ashamed, you know, that my brother was so weak. I wondered what you'd think of me."

"Hey!" I interjected. "I wouldn't judge you like that. His actions were his, not yours. And addiction's an illness we've all been touched by."

He raised his eyes to meet mine. "I *am* sorry. I had a lot to learn about addiction and suicide. What I mean is, I had a lot of shame around what happened. It took me a while to figure out it wasn't my shame to carry."

We clinked our brandy glasses together. "To no shame," I toasted. "Glad to see you, bro." And I was.

Within a couple of weeks, it was like he had never left. We hung out together all the time. I discovered Justin was once again enviably in the know, bringing me along to parties populated by models or dinners with titans of industry. He seemed to know everyone and everyone seemed to like him. I genuinely did too, so it wasn't a surprise. Some people just have that kind of radiance. Justin came back from the dead and infused new life into mine.

This new life crystalized one magic night. This was back in the days before Justin and I launched Convincer, and after the most unlikely of events: a company outing consisting of paintball warfare designed to build office camaraderie.

After hours of running around in the heat getting shot at, I was frustrated and irritable. A squib landed squarely in my abdomen and exploded yellow paint. I feigned a dramatic collapse to the ground. "Tell Betty I love her," I gasped out, playing along but secretly relieved to be "dead." *Enough of this shit.*

Justin dropped to my side. "Noooooo!" he howled. "Not the cap!" He fired off a series of rounds. Rainbows of paint spattered in every direction as boiler-suit-clad players fired back.

Justin shouldn't even have been a part of this ridiculous exercise, but for my boss's spontaneous offer at a bar where we had all found one another earlier that week. I didn't really think much about it; after all, his ability to solicit this kind of invitation was part of Justin's magic. Part of the reason I relished being in his orbit.

I can't say if shooting paintballs at colleagues resulted in increased trust or morale for others. For me, it brought a shocking number of bruises, as well as the disturbing recognition of a cutthroat competitiveness among my coworkers.

We were all supposed to meet up for dinner after breaking for showers and a change. I was sore and irritable and wanted to go home, but I knew that wouldn't be viewed well by my boss, an overly enthusiastic type named Len. I thought of some of the assholes I worked with and how they had revealed their natures out on that dusty field earlier in the day. Suddenly, I was sick of the whole thing. The corporate culture, even one with open-plan office, cappuccino bar, and "fun" team-building exercises, felt like a yoke.

By the time I arrived at the Brazilian steakhouse for dinner, I was in a foul temper. I hovered outside and lit a cigarette, the first I'd had in months. The acrid smoke curled into my palate with a familiar glorious rush of satisfaction tainted by shame.

"I know you got killed today. But that doesn't mean you literally have to kill yourself." Justin plucked the cigarette from my fingers. "Okay?" he asked and then ground out the butt on the cement without waiting for my response.

I knew how he hated smoking, one of his brother Tommy's many self-destructive vices, so I didn't protest.

"What's up, man?" Justin inquired. "Are you mad I crashed your party?" He looked genuinely anxious that he might have offended me.

"God no, J. You're completely welcome. In fact, you're welcome to it."

"Do I sense an existential crisis coming on?" Justin's tone was serious but his eyes were merry.

"You know my plan," I replied. "Right now I'm just struggling with the patience it requires."

"You do work with a ton of jerks."

A burst of laughter escaped me. "You picked up on that way faster than I did."

Justin shrugged. "I had no skin in the game."

We stood there in a companionable silence, watching cars rush past on the avenue in front of us. The traffic lights cycled through one round and then another.

"Let's get out of here," Justin finally said.

"Len won't be happy with me," I protested half-heartedly.

Justin fixed me with a knowing stare. "You don't give a fuck what Len thinks. Besides, I have a proposition for you. Maybe the path to being your own boss is shorter than you think."

A grin transformed his face; those bright eyes sparkled in the dusk. "Let's go talk it over, Will. Just say yes."

Justin and I talked all night. He opened up about what he'd been working on since arriving back in L.A., a subject on which he had been previously quite mysterious.

Justin told me that in his last job he'd resolved a problem with a key piece of coding for a software company he'd been working for in Silicon Valley. He wasn't even on the tech side; he was in finance, but he took a look one day when the engineers were stumped and worked it out. The head of the company credited Justin with turning their fortunes around and he got a huge bonus. Then he quit, determined to forge his own path. He came away with the respect of Warren Sax, his former boss, who was now poised to become the majority investor in Justin's company.

Justin had all the elements lined up for the launch of a virtual reality company. Sax would back the R&D and initial launch, proprietary technology developed by a leader in the field, a business plan including marketing he claimed would revolutionize this burgeoning aspect of entertainment.

As a longtime gamer, I was more than intrigued, I was dumbstruck. And even more so by Justin's offer to not only put me on salary, but also give me a sweat-equity financial stake in the company.

"I owe you and I trust you," he said simply when I protested he was being overly generous.

I gave notice the next morning.

Looking around the Pickford now, I spot a few of our employees. Sunil and his wife, Jahnvi, cluster with Parker and his boyfriend, Curtis. Faroud chats up Annie's friends Bella and Felicia, while socially awkward Dylan, our "resident genius," as Justin always called him, hangs on the edges, trying to insert himself into the conversation.

I am responsible for these people. They trust me. I'm not sure I can make this company survive without Justin by my side. My "plan" to be my own boss seems naïve and foolish now.

Panic wraps its steel grip around my heart. My forehead is suddenly damp with sweat. I mop my brow with a cocktail napkin. Take a sip of my drink.

More people filter into the bar. A few gather around Justin's photograph. Annie stares glassily ahead. The tone is hushed and somber; more alcohol is needed to loosen tongues and lighten moods.

A few murmured words to Molly and she's in action, taking drink orders and getting them filled. She tries hard, Molly.

I decide I can't think about her right now.

A couple I vaguely recognize comes over to offer condolences to Annie. She composes her face politely. They correctly assume I'm Justin's business partner. They tell me to take good care of Annie. They drift away, their relief at having the painful moment out of the way evident on both their faces.

I remember who they are. The CEO of the company where Annie works, Vern Fellowes, and his second wife. Under other circumstances I would have loved to have talked to him. I'm fascinated with how his company, MediFutur, is using VR tech to train physicians and surgeons. Today I'm not sure I could hold up my end of the conversation, so it's just as well they moved on.

A little while later, I notice the wife has taken off her blazer and unbuttoned the top three buttons on her silk blouse. She slips one nylon-clad foot free from a black satin pump and runs it up her husband's leg. Funerals make people horny. I've seen it before. Maybe it's the desire to reaffirm life in the most primal way. Maybe it's the booze.

CHAPTER TWELVE

CAROL

Justin became my world. I didn't make a conscious decision about it, but once it was just the two of us, it seemed the only natural path.

I had friends, of course, but I didn't socialize much and I certainly didn't date. My boy had already lost so many people, the last thing I wanted was to bring anyone transient into his life.

I did sneak off on the occasional night out when he had a sleepover at a friend's house. I'd go into the city and pick up some guy in town on business, sleep with him in his hotel, and then disappear back to Long Island. I became a different woman on those occasions, using made-up names and stories; one time I was "Corinne from Calabasas," another time "Carla from Cleveland," a third, "Cara from Clearwater, Kansas."

I liked the alliteration, and keeping the names close to Carol helped me keep my lies straight.

I ached for the physical release, longed for the touch of a man's hands on my body, desperately wanted to be held. But more than that, I needed to disappear into someone else for a few hours. In these encounters, I wasn't Carol, a tragic figure around whom loved ones seemed to die with terrifying force and frequency. I wasn't the single mother of a son I felt ill equipped to raise on my own.

Sometimes I laughed out loud thinking about how the people in my office or at Justin's school would react if they saw me, smoky eyed and predatory, prowling around an anonymous hotel bar. On these excursions, I looked different, felt different, *was* different, and I returned home a little more able to cope. I'm only human, after all.

Mostly though, I embraced my role. I gave my child love and stability. He would know that the dangerous world also had safe harbors. I would never miss an opportunity to tell him, "I love you."

He was a good son in return. He was smart and did well in school. He charmed students and teachers alike. Other moms complained about slamming doors, eye rolls, and talking back, but Justin didn't give me any of that grief. Ever since that day in the car after his last school fight, we had operated as a team.

I riffle through memories. Justin's election to middle school student council on a platform of "less homework, better cafeteria food," the two of us laughing and joking as we inked signs onto oaktag. How as captain, he led the debate team to statewide championships, with me cheering in the stands. The time he knew he could trust me when a kid was sick from drinking. After I got the kid cleaned up and safely home, Justin informed me, "I told them you'd be cool. I knew it. I knew you'd just say yes." I couldn't help but feel a thrill of pride at his faith in me.

The week he turned fourteen, Justin surpassed me in height. He was absurdly delighted by this milestone, which in turn delighted me. A few weeks later I caught him inspecting his bare chest in the bathroom mirror and realized he was searching for hairs.

My boy was turning into a man, right before my eyes. I was gripped with a poignant sense of loss that surprised me. Surely this was what I wanted, my boy to grow up, become a man, and have a full life. The kind of long, rich expanse of existence denied to so many in our family.

But my identity was now firmly rooted in the role of *Justin's mother*. I was other things, of course—a real estate agent, a friend, a committee member, occasionally a recklessly wanton stranger—but my role as his mother defined me. Everything else was carved around that. He was the shiny object around which my world revolved. What would happen to me when that focus and structure evaporated?

There I was, mourning the loss of his *childhood*. That seems shallow now in retrospect as here I am, once again, Carol the tragic figure.

Yet another very pretty girl comes over to me to offer her condolences. I sometimes wonder how Annie stood it, Justin's magnetic pull on people. People flocked to him, not just women, but certainly he never lacked in that department. From an early age, he was a charmer.

If I'm no longer Justin's mother, who am I?

I have no idea.

CHAPTER THIRTEEN

ANNIE

Justin and I grew closer, our lives more enmeshed. We spent tons of time with Will and whichever woman he was currently dating. We formed a new crowd of regulars, mostly people that worked at Convincer and MediFutur. Our friends blended, but they also didn't. As some friends fell away and other friendships shifted, I reassured myself these kinds of changes were totally normal for a new couple setting out to conquer the world together. Justin liked the idea of a "synergy" between our careers. I liked it too; I felt like we were a power couple in our expanding circle.

And I was dizzy and dazed with love. I wondered how his genes would mesh with mine, what our babies would look like.

That final night in New York had ended without a proposal. After we put his mother in a car to take her home, Justin and I walked through the thrumming streets of Manhattan, arms linked. We got back to our hotel, nuzzled and fumbled our way into drunken sex, and passed out.

The next morning, I harbored a twinge of wistful disappointment, but Justin was so damn pleased with how the whole visit had gone that I tucked it away, rationalizing that a proposal after a date with his mother was hardly the romantic ideal anyway.

Also, we'd not even been together four months. I was surprised by my own blinding focus on a proposal and marriage, and told myself to cool my jets. Everything was going perfectly; there was absolutely no reason for me to get needy about locking it down.

Nonetheless, the mental gymnastics I indulged in after we got back from New York are embarrassing to remember. I tried to balance open receptivity with a policy of no expectations, but I felt compelled to relentlessly parse Justin's every text and all of our verbal conversations. I became fixated on potential hidden meanings, and focused on minute fluctuations in his behavior. I didn't dare confess this lunacy to even my closest friends. I knew it was nutty, but I couldn't stop.

I went to work, saw Justin, socialized with friends, even poured some of my angst into a short story. But it was as if I was surrounded by a magnetic field of obsession that buzzed continuously even while I was seemingly going about my ordinary life.

obsession [əbˈ-se-shen]
   noun, compulsive preoccupation with a fixed idea or an unwanted feeling or emotion, often accompanied by feelings of anxiety

Bella called me on it one day out of the blue. I was always particularly careful how I talked about Justin around her, since even if she kept her mouth shut, a roll of the eyes or a shrug could reveal her ambivalence about him. But one Thursday when we met up for a girls' night out, she lit into me almost as soon as we ordered our first cocktail. I was "absent even when I was present," and "completely losing myself in my relationship." She was right, of course, but I defended myself and him.

She backed off. I apologized if I'd left her feeling abandoned of late. We ordered another round and some food and parted with our usual hug at the end of the night.

I reasoned that while Bella was right about how wrapped up in Justin I was, she was also a little jealous: solidly single, and her last few dates had been disasters. This was just the inevitable kind of shift that occurred in friendships as people coupled up.

One Saturday night near the end of the summer, Justin took me to a restaurant/bar perched on the rooftop of a DTLA hotel. He secured our drinks and found us a spot to lean on against the wall circling the western edge of the bar.

The sun hung big and orange, smoldering its way down to the horizon. Signage reared large, advertising tequila, soda, and fast food, set against a cityscape of mixed architecture: classic deco; rehabbed factories; striking, shiny new columns of glass and steel.

I glanced down over the wall. It was almost five feet high, but the drop to the empty lot below was sheer and straight, and I felt a little queasy. A glass dropped over its edge would shatter explosively. I lifted my drink away from its resting place on the edge and when I spotted a pair of barstools opening up on the other side of the roof, I nabbed them.

The cocktails were strong, the crowd around us boisterous. We were having a great time, laughing with strangers, a usual night out with Justin. When Bella showed up, I was a little tipsy and I thought it was a happy coincidence. But then I saw Will threading through the crowd with some of the other guys from their office. Next I spotted Felicia and her sister. Then my work wife, Hayley Hayter, along with a few other friends from my office. Then my mom and stepfather. My heart began to thud wildly.

This was just like Justin. An element of surprise. The assemblage of all the people he and I loved best in the world. When I saw Carol arrive, I knew. Tonight was the night. My face went hot. Justin cupped my jaw in the palm of his hand and whispered, "I love you, Annie O' My Heart."

He spun away and with a wave of his hand, the sound system blaring alt-rock cut out. A gong chimed, pure and true, its resonance shimmering in the hot evening air. The crowd assembled on the rooftop drew silent.

I found Bella's eyes and she grinned at me, raising her mojito in a toast.

Justin began to speak. "Now that I have your attention, friends and soon-to-be friends, let me explain. Standing with us mere mortals on this rooftop is a goddess. A woman I was lucky enough to rescue from a car crash, never knowing that she would be the one to crash my heart wide open."

He had everyone's attention. Why not? He was gorgeous, magnetic, *magic*. I couldn't believe I was the focus of this public display of affection by this beautiful man. My face went hot. I sipped at my spicy, fruity drink. My mother patted me on the back.

Justin leapt up on a low glass cocktail table as a startled couple swept their glasses out of his way with good-natured laughs.

Out of the corner of my eye, I saw Carol pop a pill from a prescription vial.

"Annie Elizabeth Hendrix," Justin intoned, "will you do me the extraordinary honor of becoming my wife?"

The moment I had been dreaming of for so long, here at last. I savored it, taking a breath and letting my eyes scan the crowd around me. Friends, family, and strangers all beamed at me, silently urging me to proclaim my acceptance.

"What? Is that a hesitation?" Justin exclaimed. "Don't break my heart!"

The crowd gasped as Justin sprung from the cocktail table and up onto the ledge of the wall overlooking that sheer drop to the vacant lot below. My stomach lurched.

"Get down from there, you idiot!" I shouted. "Of course I'll marry you."

"That's a relief." Justin grinned at me. "Will, my friend, the ring, please."

Will tossed Justin a small black velvet box. I watched what happened next as if it occurred in slow motion. The box sailed past Justin's outstretched hand and over the edge of the wall. Everyone gasped.

Some dude in a muscle tee guffawed. "Good aim, asshole."

Justin shrugged. "Better get that," he announced, before springing off the wall and plummeting over the edge. More gasps! A couple of screams split the air, one of them possibly my own.

Momentarily frozen to the spot, I watched Justin disappear from view. Then my muscles woke and I raced across the width of the rooftop, knocking people and cocktails ruthlessly out of my path.

This can't be happening. This can't be happening. The refrain pounded like a drumbeat in my brain.

Heart thudding in my chest, I peered over the edge expecting to see Justin's broken remains.

My eyes adjusted. I blinked. Justin stood erect on the base of an inflatable slide, completely unharmed. He flipped over the huge piece of cardboard he was holding as soon as he caught my eye. It read:

JUST SAY YES

Justin couldn't propose in an ordinary way. Of course not! No quiet dinner for two with a ring concealed in the chocolate mousse, or a sunset beachside sinking to one knee. The proposal he delivered was epic, totally Justin. Adrenaline skyrocketed through my system, a result of shock, joy, excitement, and hope. I was furious and relieved. But mainly ecstatic, so I tamped down the tiny tendrils of trepidation that gnawed at me.

Would I love the unpredictability of being married to this man? Or would it leave me perpetually on edge and shaken?

The party on the rooftop afterward raged into the early hours. The ring was perfect, an antique I had admired in a jewelry shop in Brentwood weeks before. We danced and hugged and cried, friends and strangers alike.

I couldn't remember ever feeling so happy. Life with Justin would always be an adventure, and even though I was a little afraid of that, I resolutely decided it was exactly what I needed.

CHAPTER FOURTEEN

WILL

We were living like rock stars. No, that's a lie. We were living lean and pouring all of our time and energy into building our company. But we *felt* like rock stars.

Our office was in Venice, close to the beach and the boardwalk, located in the former home of a gone-bust company that sold ridiculously expensive organic baby clothes (a fact I discerned upon discovering a discarded box of rompers, or whatever those one-piece things that babies wear are called, each one tagged for $285 retail). *For fuck's sake, they were each the size of a handkerchief.*

The walls of the office were painted pale pink and powder blue (very old-school gender normative), and the wall-to-wall carpet was a cheerful but impractical pale yellow. Justin negotiated a reduced rent in return for not insisting the landlord repaint. We were so busy we stopped noticing pretty quickly.

We converted one half of the floor into a design and test lab; the other side was creative development, marketing and sales, finance and accounting. We added employees every day, gearing up for the launch of our first product, a virtual reality system offering haptic technology superior to anything on the market.

In layman's terms, we were building a system that allowed the user to touch and interact with avatars and objects within the virtual reality experience in an unparalleled way.

Gamers would be able to heft swords, smash vases, shake hands with characters (maybe even kiss them, although that was a subject of a fierce office-wide debate on the ethics of AI interaction), all relying on proprietary technology that promised the user unprecedented realism within their virtual reality.

I was pumped. We were going to be changing the very nature of gaming. I didn't understand all the technical details, but I knew I was happier than I'd ever been.

Shackles had been cut from my wrists and ankles. I was building something I believed in, and I couldn't believe my good fortune. If Justin and I hadn't randomly met briefly all those years ago back when we were both just starting business school, if he hadn't remembered my (pretty normal) acts of friendship toward him so fondly, if he hadn't decided to come back to L.A. after finishing up his MBA in New York, if, if, if . . .

Those early days were heady. We took pride in putting together a talented team and Justin's enthusiasm and energy spilled over onto everyone. We all knew that we were making entertainment, but we were lit up with a messianic glow, convinced somehow that we were also fulfilling some extraordinary higher purpose. We worked hard and played hard together, becoming regulars at a rotation of local places, forming deep friendships as we built the company.

Molly appears in front of me with a refresh of my drink. She really is a great girl. I'm man enough to recognize that my irritation with her isn't really about her at all. I pull her in for a quick squeeze and a kiss.

The launch, Convincer's long-sought goal, is now only weeks away. Dread lodges in my gut, and a shudder passes through my body. *Can I pull this off alone?*

CHAPTER FIFTEEN

CAROL

I devoted my life to protecting my son and yet here I am at his funeral. Yet more proof that life is both painfully short and tragically unpredictable.

In fact, in my experience, it's exactly when you think you've got a situation wired that the fates throw a curveball to keep you on your toes.

One such example: When Justin was just shy of seventeen, his class took an "outdoor education" trip to the Catskill Mountains. For them, four full days of tugging ropes and swatting insects. For me, four full days of freedom from my role of "Justin's mother."

I arranged to take the days off work. Booked myself a hotel room in the city. I wasn't just thinking about prowling for a pickup, although that was penciled in to my agenda. I also bought a ticket for a Broadway matinee, and planned to do a little shopping. Mostly I relished the idea of being alone and anonymous in the midst of the buzzing New York hive.

My first day had been entirely satisfactory. I dropped Justin off at his bus and drove right to my hotel, where I had arranged early check-in. I took a long, luxurious bath in the spa tub in my suite, and then went for a walk, soaking up the energy of the city. I stayed hidden behind sunglasses and didn't engage much with other people. When I did, to buy a sandwich at a deli or to inquire about the price of a scarf, I adopted a vague accent and pretended I spoke limited English.

I was hiding in plain sight and I loved it. That night in the hotel, I ordered room service and watched movies, went to bed early and slept well.

The next day was more of the same. I went to the Met and wandered the permanent collection, then walked for miles, happily observing the street theater in Manhattan: vendors selling knockoff designer purses, tiny well-dressed ladies-who-lunch toting tiny, equally well-dressed dogs, briskly moving businessmen, determined-looking suit-clad women going even faster than the men *and* in heels, a rainbow coalition of nannies with their young charges, a string of schoolchildren crossing a street escorted by their teachers and linked together by a bright purple rope.

I was deeply and happily in my solitude when my phone rang. The caller ID revealed a number I didn't recognize. Some primal instinct overrode my temptation to simply dismiss the call. "Hello?" I answered with some trepidation.

"Carol, this is Ronna Markson from the high school. Justin is fine, but . . ."

My breath snagged on the word *but*. "What's wrong? What's happened?" The words shot from my mouth.

"He's fine. He's got a gash on his head, but we've been to the emergency room and they were able to close it with butterfly stitches. He's fine," she repeated. "But we don't think he should stay for the rest of the trip. *Just in case* he has a mild concussion. He's *fine*."

I checked out of the hotel immediately. Got in my car and drove. Over the course of the three-plus-hour journey to the kids' campground, I fretted over Justin's well-being. I also irrationally excoriated myself for trying to escape the responsibility of my child, even briefly. I know now it didn't make sense, but somehow I convinced myself that if I had stayed at home in my identity as "Justin's mother," none of this would have happened.

By the time I reached the campsite, tired, stressed, guilty, bladder bursting, I was on the verge of tears, which fell freely as soon as I saw my boy. Pale faced and lacking his usual exuberance, a thick white bandage covering half of his forehead, he seemed frail, young, and vulnerable.

"Oh, baby," I crooned, pulling him into my arms. "Poor thing. How did it happen?"

Justin didn't respond, but Ronna did. "Some of the other boys say he started it, actually, throwing rocks, acting like a bully. He got hit when one of them fought back."

"Did you see him start it?" I demanded, my blood instantly boiling.

"Uh, no, but . . ."

"I see," I said coldly. "You're very willing to believe these other boys over Justin, aren't you? My son is the one with the head wound, and somehow he's the problem? Clearly, you don't know my son very well. He is incapable of being a bully."

I glanced over at Justin. I could see the hurt in his eyes, the wounded embarrassment at this false accusation. "Come on, baby, we're leaving," I soothed him. "I won't let you spend another minute here."

Ronna was also eager for us to get on our way, bringing over a release form for me to sign and Justin's packed rucksack. "You shouldn't drive all the way back tonight," she suggested. "There's a motel in town that's not too bad."

"This isn't over," I hissed at her as we departed. "I won't have my boy unjustly accused."

We found the motel, a creaky, weather-beaten place with a tiny diner attached. I rented one room with two beds for us to share; I didn't want to let Justin out of my sight. He put up a protest, but I suspected he was secretly relieved.

Over grilled cheese and fries in the diner, I asked again about the events that led to his injury. With his eyes ducked shyly down, Justin told me how he'd defended a smaller kid from one of the class bullies, stepping in to physically block an assault. The bully backed off in the moment, but later ambushed Justin, pelting him with rocks until he was bloody. The kids who saw the attack were too scared to help, and lied to avoid being the next victims.

"I knew it!" I declared triumphantly. "I knew you couldn't have been the instigator." I was outraged. I wanted Justin to name names. I wanted the bully who'd attacked my son expelled from the school, and the kids who lied to protect the bully forced to tell the truth. But Justin refused to give me the names. He pled with me, insisting it would be worse for him if he ratted.

"I have power now, Mom, don't you see? I have something over him."

"That's ridiculous," I replied. "I don't know what kind of

power you think you get from shielding him. Yes, it's important to stand up to bullies and I'm glad you did, but you don't then protect them."

Justin shut down. His spine went rigid. He cracked his neck with crisp precision. Finished his meal in silence and crawled into his bed in our motel room as soon as dinner was over. I stayed up most of the night, setting an alarm to ring every two hours so I could doze a bit but also keep an eye on Justin.

Our drive back home the next morning continued our conversational standoff. Justin would discuss anything with me but the details leading to his assault. If I brought it up in any way, shape, or form, he shut me down.

Once we were crossing the threshold of our townhouse, he turned to me and gripped me in a hug. Now that he was taller than me and wider too, we fit together more awkwardly than when he was a little boy, but his scent still felt more like home to me than any physical place.

"Thank you for coming to get me. Now promise you won't ask me about the names ever again."

I protested, insisting that as his mother I had a right to know, that the school had an obligation to prevent bullying, that other students could be in danger, but no argument I made swayed him. I disagreed with him, but also felt a grudging admiration for the strength of character he was showing, his determination to handle his problems on his own. I decided to let it go.

I'm pulled from this memory by someone I don't recognize offering me a plate of food. A hamburger and fries, piled high and greasy.

The smell takes me right back to that night in the diner and turns my stomach. It was the first time I know of that Justin kept a secret from me, but I also know it was not the last.

CHAPTER SIXTEEN

ANNIE

After we were engaged, I became thoroughly swept up in the same kind of bridal frenzy I'd seen descend on any number of my peers.

I became fixated on my dress. I boldly commissioned an avant-garde designer friend of Justin's to make me *a confection,* and then squirmed in frustration as I thought the dress he designed was *all wrong, would never fit properly, would never be done in time, would be a disaster!*

My sky-high expectations for the dress seemed to come from my deeply hidden hope that I would be *enough* for Justin, which itself, of course, signaled to me that I wasn't and never would be. I pushed this all aside though, and let myself get swept up in the whirl. What bride wants to believe she *isn't* enough for her groom?

> **enough [i-ˈnəf]**
>   ***adjective,*** sufficient to fill a need or desire
>   **synonyms:** adequate, acceptable, satisfying, suitable
>   **antonyms:** insufficient, inadequate, deficient

Besides my dress obsession, I was absorbed in pre-wedding trials, tribulations, and delights: narrowing the guest list (Justin wanted to invite everyone in the world, it seemed), picking bridesmaids (and their attire), asking my stepdad to walk me down the aisle, choosing an officiant, flowers, a menu, music, and a pompously tiered cake.

I asked Bella to be my maid of honor at a champagne-soaked lunch at a Malibu restaurant overlooking the Pacific Ocean. We both cried a little and hugged a lot. She promised to love Justin as much as she loved me and then threw herself into the role, planning my shower, organizing spa and beauty appointments, and holding my hand through every little crisis. I resolved to leave any of her past voiced concerns about our relationship behind.

I was also super busy at work and had several friends' weddings to attend, including two destination affairs that Justin and I attended together (Maui and Cabo), so it felt like the eleven months between Justin's epic proposal and our actual wedding day flew by in a blur of preparation and anticipation.

Five weeks before our wedding, a heartwrenching story broke on the local news. A notoriously eccentric old woman by the name of Birdie Tonks died in her Hancock Park home. Even though she was wealthy, with both money and four children, she died totally alone save for her twenty-six cats.

The animals were practically feral; Birdie had apparently been in decline for some time and none of her kids came by much, if at all, in the months, and possibly the years, before her death.

I knew Birdie a little. We volunteered at the same animal shelter. She was kooky, sweet, a little frail. I always liked her, but I also didn't think much about it when she stopped volunteering. People came and went all the time. I also had no idea she was an "heiress," which I learned watching news footage of her corpse being carried from her mansion on a stretcher.

When her youngest daughter discovered her mother, Birdie had been dead for over a week. The discovery of the body brought forth the three other siblings, eager to pick over their mother's estate. While Birdie's four children found their own petty squabbles to engage in (there was both gossip and lawsuits), they were equally eager to dispose of the "kids," which was how Birdie referred to her beloved cats.

Word got around our network of animal rescue volunteers. Many of the cats were older; most of them faced certain death if they went into a shelter. One Wednesday night, over a dinner of take-out ramen, when I was trying to get Justin to make a decision about his boutonniere, a frantic text conversation began circulating. Word was, the cats were going to be put into a shelter by the end of the week unless someone offered to take them.

My distress over this news took my appetite away. "How can people be so heartless?" I demanded. "What's wrong with them? I never even heard Birdie *mention* her actual children, but she talked about her *kids* all the time."

"You can't save everyone and everything, Annie," Justin said. "Even though it's a noble trait and one of the reasons I love you." He smiled at me. "Anyway. What would we do with twenty-six more cats? For that matter, think how traumatized Cinnamon Toast would be. Used to being the favorite for so long—mass adoption would be a crippling blow. She'd need kitty therapy."

C.T.'s tail twitched in agreement. "It's just so sad," I replied. "But maybe we'll be able to figure something out," I added, "we" referring to my text group of shelter volunteers. "Everyone's going to reach out and we'll reconnect tomorrow. We'll place as many as we can."

"We're getting married in five weeks."

I looked at Justin quizzically. "Tell me something I don't know."

"I'm just saying. We're going on a honeymoon and we already have C.T. to board. It's not the time for another cat." He kissed me then, long and deep. When we broke apart, he committed to a delicate purple orchid for his lapel on our wedding day.

The next day I had to review materials for one of Medi-Futur's most promising new products, a virtual reality heart surgery program that would allow surgeons to train while experiencing the *actual sensations* they would feel in the operating room.

The resistance of flesh and muscle, the delicacy of working around veins and arteries, all of the complexities of the surgery as if done on a living, breathing person (along with built-in complications that could be programmed with the touch of a button). Surgeons could experience these sensations over and over again without putting an actual human life at risk.

We were launching the product at a big medical convention in Las Vegas. My job had been partly prepping the material for the launch (press release, posters, banners, product specs, demonstration videos, etc.) and partly keeping any whisper about the product from getting out *before* the launch. My bosses wanted to make a big splash in Vegas.

Proofs for the specs had come back riddled with typos. I was already in a shitty mood over Birdie Tonks's cats. I wanted to get home to Justin and so tucked the specs into my tote, figuring no one would ever be the wiser.

Then to my horror, in the elevator leaving the office I ran into Hayley Hayter, the very person who'd emphasized the importance of keeping MediFutur's proprietary material on-site. I was sure Hayley must have thought something was seriously wrong with me, I was so awkward.

Now I was at our kitchen table plowing through the mistakes with a red pen and a mounting sense of rage at other people's incompetence, resentful that I'd had to bring so much work home, uneasy about sneaking the specs out of the office.

A long, frustrating night loomed ahead of me, after a gulped take-out dinner, during which both Justin and I had been distracted.

I let out a long sigh.

Justin came up behind me and put his hands on my shoulders. "Wow. You're tense." He began to give me a massage.

I shrugged him off. "Not now, sorry."

"What is that you're working on, anyway?"

I covered the specs with my arm. "Sorry, top secret!" I tried to keep my voice light, but I knew I sounded strained. "I'm sorry, sweetheart," I capitulated. "But I can't share. All you need to know is that they're such a fucking mess I'm going to be at this for hours."

"I'll leave you to it then."

I could hear the hurt in his voice. I turned and pulled him back toward me for a kiss. "I'm sorry, baby. I promise I'll make it up to you later."

He ran his hand up my neck and twined it in my hair in a way he knew made me hot for him. "And I promise to take you up on that."

Another kiss and Justin left me alone. I went back to work.

A couple of hours later, my phone began to blow up. One text after the next. I set my pen down and checked my cell.

Did you hear? An anonymous donor got all of Birdie's cats a home on a farm in Chino!

Whaaaaaat? Great news!

Any idea who it was?

Not one of her stupid kids, that's for sure. They should all rot in hell. Cat killers.

Look on the bright side. At least the kids were saved!

Yes!

My terrible mood evaporated, just like that.

"You'll never guess," I bubbled, bursting in on Justin in the bedroom. He looked up in surprise from the book he was reading. I proceeded to share: all of the cats saved, and kept together too. On a farm! "It's what Birdie would have wanted. I'm so glad."

"I did it for you," Justin said. I blinked at him. I had no idea what he was talking about. "I relocated the cats," he continued. "You were so upset about it and I can't have my beautiful bride stressed out before our wedding, can I? Work is twisting you up enough as it is."

"You're kidding me, right? Joking?"

"Absolutely not," he declared, looking slightly offended. "I thought it would make you happy. I meant it as kind of a wedding gift." He crossed his arms over his chest.

"Oh my god, J, I love it! It was just so unexpected. And you sprung it on me so casually . . ." I stopped talking and opened his crossed arms. Snuggled in against his broad chest. Kissed him full on the mouth. "You. Are. Amazing. How did you manage it?"

"I'm not giving away all my secrets yet. Wait until we're married."

"Seriously, J. Thank you so much. This means so much to me. I don't know how to repay you."

"We don't have to make a big deal out of it, okay? I don't need a parade." He slid his hand up the back of my thigh. "But as I recall, you already had a promise to make good on."

His hand went higher and soon we were tangled in each other, heated and urgent.

Later, I considered texting my shelter volunteer group the amazing news of Justin's generosity, but hesitated and eventually decided against it. Justin was funny about things sometimes; I recognized this. He kept certain parts of his life compartmentalized. Saving Birdie's cats was an act of love that he had performed for me, and a component of the gift was that he didn't need anyone's recognition of his act but mine. I filed the gesture away, one more piece of solid proof of Justin's love.

CHAPTER SEVENTEEN

WILL

Arriving at the office for one of our usual Saturday afternoon catch-ups, I was shocked to find Justin in tears. He quickly wiped his eyes and sauntered over to the coffee maker so his back was to me. Wanting to respect his desire to conceal his distress, I set down the greasy bag containing the two burritos I'd nabbed on the way in and offered a casual "good afternoon," as if I hadn't noticed a thing.

Justin hadn't indicated anything was wrong. Not last night when we partied (another Friday night of free-flowing drinks and fast new friends at a local bar), or earlier today when I'd texted to confirm his burrito order. I couldn't remember seeing him this upset since his brother had died.

When he turned back from the counter with cups of coffee for both of us, all traces of his tears were erased. We chowed down, drank coffee, discussed the week's progress, the challenges that lay ahead. We cracked jokes about the perils of double-dating a pair of identical twins we'd met the night before.

There was something somber operating beneath the surface, though, as hard as Justin tried to mask it. His ebullient spirit was so much the lifeblood of the company, I was worried, not just for my friend, but for all of us.

It was only when we were walking out into the pink-streaked dusk that I broached it. "You all right, man?" I inquired casually. "You need anything?"

To my surprise, Justin laughed, a full-throated bellow that shook his entire body. "You know me too well," he affirmed. "I think I could get away with hiding it from most people, but not you. This is why you're my main man."

Glad as I was to see his good humor return, I had to press deeper. "What's up?" I asked softly. "Is it something to do with the business?"

"Sort of."

My stomach knotted with apprehension. "Come on, J, what the hell does 'sort of' mean? I'm a minority owner, but I'm an owner too. And I'm the one here every damn day with you. If something's going on, I need to know."

The low glare of the western leaning sun blocked me from seeing his eyes. I couldn't mistake his sigh, though, heavy and full of sadness.

"I thought I could sort it out myself. And I think I have, but not how I'd like."

The knots in my belly twisted tighter. "Sort what out?"

Justin sighed again. "You know we launched with Sax as our majority investor and another minority investor. An 80/20 split."

"Of course. Get to the point."

"Our minority investor never actually came through. I tried

to keep the negotiations going for months, while frantically looking for a replacement. Sax was getting impatient with the delay in the balance of the funding . . ."

I had to interrupt. "How could you keep this from me?"

Justin looked at me with astonishment. "It's my end of the deal. I bring in the money and oversee tech development. You run day-to-day ops and marketing. Did I make you report to me about every snag you hit?"

"No, of course not. But what does this mean for us exactly? Where are we at now? J, you were *crying*. What the fuck is going on?"

"All right. I found a minority investor. It's Carol."

"Your *mother*?" That was the last thing I expected him to say.

"She called this morning to tell me she's putting her town-house on the market to give me the money as gap financing. I didn't want to take it at first; all she's got is that place, but she insisted. I believe we'll make her money down the line, but it'll take every penny she'll make on the sale to make Sax happy, and even then we might come up a little short . . ."

My brain spun with relief. A loss of one minority investor, but so what? We'd make Carol money instead! I'd met Justin's mother a few times when she'd come out to visit. A small woman with a large personality, clearly devoted to Justin: I'd liked her.

"Why don't I invest the balance?" The offer sprang out spontaneously but was genuinely meant. I'd offered when we launched, but Justin had refused. He'd insisted that my small equity position was part of my compensation package. And since I was pulling in less than I had been at my old job I was happy to keep my savings intact and take the sweat-equity position on offer.

But now my heart was in this company; my money might as well be too. And if we could keep some of Carol's nest egg safe in the bargain? So much the better. Justin had been so generous with me; I wanted to return the favor.

Justin was reluctant, but I finally prevailed. I put together a consortium of investors that included me, my mother, and my two uncles. Together we took a small piece of the company, allowing Carol the ability to squirrel away a decent rainy day sum while still investing as well. Win-win-win, right?

Or so I thought at the time.

People are drifting out of the bar; some stop to bid Annie or Carol farewell, many just meander out into the sunshine, relieved to be done with their obligation, eager to escape to happier activities. Stories were told and laughed at, food and drink consumed, Justin honored, remembered, mourned. Now we move on. It's the way of things, right?

Molly hands me another glass of amber liquid. "In honor of your commitment to getting stinking drunk," she announces cheerfully.

I accept the glass with a frown. I don't remember voicing that intent out loud, although it's conceivable that I did.

Taking a sip, I miss, the glass chiming into a tooth, scotch spilling down my chin.

I see a knot of our closest friends gather around the memory book laid out on the bar. It feels strange that Warren Sax isn't here.

Another flicker of unease crosses my gut. I gulp more scotch.

I notice Annie's cousin Lizzie edging toward her exit. She's always bragging about how she knows everyone, and I need to get ahold of Sax. I set out after her and recognize that I'm drunker than I realized.

After the dim interior of the bar, the bright sun stuns my eyes. I grab at Lizzie's elbow so sharply she yelps.

"Sorry, sorry," I mutter, sliding on my sunglasses. "Just, can you help me get ahold of someone?"

Lizzie's eyes sparkle. This is the kind of moment she lives for. "Who is it?"

"Warren Sax."

"Oooh, tricky. But reclusive tech billionaires are my specialty."

She whips out her phone. Turns away from me as she makes a call. She greets someone effusively. Then makes the request for a number for Sax. She chortles at the response. Offers thanks before ending the call with, "Yes, now we're even."

She swivels back toward me. "We have to wait a couple of minutes. Want to tell me why?"

"Not particularly."

She snorts a laugh in reply. "Have it your way. You know you'll owe me, though, right?"

Before I can reply, her phone rings. "Here he is. Didn't even take me three," she announces with smug satisfaction.

I stare at the proffered phone. I desperately need to speak to Warren Sax. I know that. But my hair prickles at the back of my neck; my hands ball into fists. I'm consumed with an urgent need to get out of here. Out of my own skin.

CHAPTER EIGHTEEN

CAROL

I don't really like to drink, but today I clutch the glass of white wine in my hand like a lifeline. The fuzzy edges alcohol provides are something I haven't been able to afford in my life; I've had to adhere to clarity, rigidity, and sacrifice.

I'm unmoored now. The thought makes me want to giggle as I imagine myself lofted upward into the sky attached to a bouquet of helium balloons like some cartoon character. I realize I'm a little tipsy.

The photograph of Justin that Will chose is a good one. He looks handsome, my son, filled with energy and joy. How we will all want to remember him.

He can't be frozen in one image for me, of course. There were so many moments, both beautiful and ugly, if I'm honest. Raising a child is an astonishing journey. Begun in love, but with a phenomenal lack of understanding of what parenting truly means, and riddled with challenges that one never sees coming.

The dichotomy between the pleasure and pain of being a

mother was never more evident than on the day of Justin's high school graduation. This is a milestone for every family; for me it was bittersweet. I was wildly proud of him. He was graduating near the top of his class. But this also meant Justin was going off to college in the fall when it had been the two of us against the world for so long. I was excited for what this new phase might bring us both, but also deeply sad and somewhat apprehensive.

The graduation ceremony in the school auditorium was charming; students played their instruments and the valedictorian's speech was genuinely funny. Justin beamed from the stage when he walked across it to receive his diploma, fist pumping when he caught my eye.

We had an early dinner afterward, just the two of us, at Justin's favorite local Italian restaurant. I ordered a glass of wine and slid it over to his side of the table. He was eager to go off and meet his friends, so I paid the bill and dropped him at the house where the grads were gathering.

The hosting parents had sent out an email. They were going to be home, but had promised to stay upstairs. The kids would be having a coed sleepover in the rec room in the basement. Snacks, water, and soda would be provided. NO BOOZE ALLOWED.

I was a realist. *Good luck with that.* But at least the kids were all staying over and not driving. I went home, took a bath, and went to bed, content that my son was safe.

A shrill ring sucked me from a deep sleep and back into the night shadows of my bedroom. It took me a few moments to recognize the sound before I fumbled to answer the phone. It was the mother of the family hosting the graduation party. There had been an accident.

My heart plummeted. "Not involving Justin," she added hurriedly. I switched on the bedside lamp. The clock on the nightstand blinked back at me: 4:12 A.M.

I gulped air. She continued. She suggested I come get Justin. He was *fine,* she emphasized, but everyone was very shook up. Eventually I got it out of her. One of the boys at the party, a junior named Nick Ambler, had climbed up to the roof of the house. And had fallen off. Or jumped. They didn't know. But Nick was dead.

I bloomed with empathy for Nick's parents even as an overwhelming sense of relief engulfed me. It wasn't *my* boy. My boy was okay.

I threw on a robe and rushed over to pick up Justin. He was white-faced and stricken. He hurtled himself into my arms without regard for who might be looking. I stroked his hair and let him cling tight. He still needed his mama and I was deeply grateful to be there for him.

We went home and I gave him a cup of hot chocolate and some buttered toast before tucking him into bed. He didn't say much and I didn't press. I assumed that in addition to the trauma of Nick's death, Justin was also probably drunk or hungover or both at this point. I figured I'd let him sleep it off and talk it through later. I took myself back to bed but found slumber elusive.

My mind kept turning to poor Nick Ambler's parents. I didn't know them well; Nick had been a year below Justin, and their younger son was still in grade school so our families' paths hadn't crossed all that much.

But I knew loss. I understood what it was like to have your life upended with one phone call. The sun rose. I showered and dressed. Peeked in on Justin and found him wide awake.

"Do you want to come with me to the Amblers'?" I asked. "I thought we might bring some food. Offer our condolences."

Justin agreed we should go. He still seemed very shaken and I thought it was brave and compassionate of him to come with me. I hoped the visit might provide some comfort to him along with the bereaved family.

We set out for the Amblers' house with a cake and a bottle of wine. Insufficient for the loss of a child to be sure, but an offering nonetheless.

Jack Ambler opened the door in response to my knock. Bags pouched underneath his eyes; he looked like he'd aged ten years since I had seen him at the high school's holiday party.

"Hi," I stammered, suddenly less sure of our welcome than I was when we set out. "I'm Carol Childs?" It came out like a question, a squeak. "This is my son, Justin."

"I know who you are," Jack said coldly. He stared at Justin with ice-blue eyes.

Clearly coming over unannounced had been a bad idea, but it was too late to retreat. "I'm so sorry," I rushed on. "About Nick. We brought some cake and a hearty red." I flourished the gifts, feeling more awkward than ever.

Desperate to recover ground, I continued on, while Jack shifted his gaze away from Justin and stared at me stonily. "I can see we came at a bad time. And I should have called first. I'm really sorry. I didn't think . . ."

Trailing off, I placed the cake box and the bottle of wine down on the welcome mat. "I'll just leave these here. I'm sorry. We didn't mean to intrude."

Jack didn't say a word. I shrugged and turned to leave, my heart pounding. That had not gone the way I had envisioned at all. I remembered Robyn yelling at me, *"Everyone deals with grief differently."* Too damn true.

We were halfway down the path when Jack's voice boomed out after us. "Some nerve you have!" I froze. Twisted my head back around to stare at him.

"Why don't you ask your son what Nick was doing on that fucking roof?" His voice shook with rage.

"What are you talking about?" I felt rooted to the spot.

"You heard me."

I looked at Justin, who shook his head and shrugged helplessly, his eyes welling with tears.

Jack picked up the bottle of wine I had left on his doorstep and hurled it toward us. An explosion of glass and deep red liquid erupted mere inches from our feet.

"Are you crazy?" I shouted. I ran for our car, pulling Justin along with me, my heart pounding, my breath ragged.

What the hell was Jack Ambler talking about? Why was he so angry?

I started the car, my hands shaking. Made sure Justin had his seatbelt on and pulled away as quickly as I could.

Jack Ambler was in shock, I concluded. And angry. Needing someone to blame. I understood all of those emotions. His rage wasn't directed at Justin in particular, just toward all of the kids that had been at a party that had resulted in his son's death.

I glanced over at Justin. He looked pale and sad. I hated seeing my lively boy so diminished. "I swear, Mom . . ." he began, eyes downcast.

"You don't have to say a thing," I interrupted. "Don't you pay any mind to Jack Ambler, honey. He's crazed with grief and doesn't know what he's saying. I know you didn't have anything to do with Nick being on that roof."

Justin's eyes flicked to mine, suddenly hopeful. "I didn't," he affirmed, nodding fervently.

"I know."

I took one hand off the wheel and laid it on the seat. Justin's hand crept into mine. We drove like that the rest of the way home. He was a high school graduate, and soon to set off into great unknowns, but in this moment, he was my little boy. It was the two of us against the world. Just like always.

I raise my glass to my lips and drain my wine. Clarity is not my friend. Rigidity has proved a useless defense against life's assaults. I've made the ultimate sacrifice. What else is there left for me to lose?

CHAPTER NINETEEN

ANNIE

I'm back at our house in Mar Vista, spectacularly, thrillingly, alone. I slam the front door behind me and twist the dead bolt closed. The cloying scent of fresh paint assaults my nostrils, so I gulp air in through my mouth.

I ran out of there, truth be told. It all became too much. I didn't even say a proper goodbye to Carol, which I feel shitty about now. I left her a message, telling her I got overwhelmed (true) and had to leave (also true). I promised I'd call her later.

I meant it at the time, but now I'm not so sure.

I kick off my shoes. Strip off the fucking Spanx. Leave my black dress in a puddle on the floor. Collapse in my underwear on the California king–size bed Justin insisted on purchasing for this, our tiny first home, and close my eyes. The bed is really too big for the room, but Justin insisted it was aspirational for our next, bigger, grander home, which was sure to include a large master suite.

That was Justin. Always dreaming and scheming. Mostly making it happen too. Mostly. Until his mangled body was pulled from a car that had skidded into an expanse of nothingness off Mulholland Drive and bounced its way down the mountainside.

I'd love to scream, but it seems like too much effort.

Cinnamon Toast leaps up onto my bed and snuggles next to me. A thin band of light snakes through the plantation shutters hanging on the bedroom window and sparks the gleam of my emerald and diamond engagement ring. I twist the antique around on my finger.

Damn you, Justin! How could you abandon me?

I wish for the sweet oblivion of sleep, but I am rigidly alert. With a sigh, I get up off the bed and open Justin's side of the closet. I haven't been able to touch any of his things since he died; I even asked Will to pick out Justin's clothes for the funeral.

Running my hand over the shoulder of Justin's favorite blazer (a buttery soft navy cashmere), I lean in to inhale his lingering scent. A fresh stab of bitter grief makes my knees weak and I stumble back, the blazer clutched in my arms.

I slip the jacket on. It swims on me in a way that I find comforting. The blazer is expensive, of excellent quality, like all the things Justin favored. I tuck my hands into the silk-lined pockets and my fingers find a crumpled slip of paper. I smooth it out and lay it on the dresser. It turns out to be a receipt for the last meal Justin and I ate out together, a favorite sushi joint. I doubt I will ever be able to eat there again.

I pull an armful of his clothes out of the closet and fling them on the bed. I shimmy into a pair of his jeans. They flap around my legs. I twist a silk tie through the belt loops and tug it tight around my waist. Digging into a front pocket, I find a handful of scratch-off lottery tickets. This brings a small smile to my face; Justin knew the odds, but he always still believed he would hit.

A shoebox brings a wallet I don't recognize, stuffed with a wad of cash. I count it, fanning the bills out onto the dresser next to the receipt: $1,500. An emergency stash? The money makes me curious. I turn out every pocket, dig behind every sweater, heaping the rest of Justin's clothes in a disorderly pile on the floor.

I find more cash, another seven grand in total. Why did Justin have so much cash squirreled away?

Then, in the inside breast pocket of his brown leather jacket, I find a feminine floral silk scarf. One that doesn't belong to me.

I finger the delicate fabric. Bring it up to my face. Inhale. It's scented with jasmine. A shudder runs through me. I recognize both the pattern and the perfume.

This scarf belongs to Hayley Hayter, a colleague of mine and a friend of us both.

I remember Justin snagging one of my scarves back in the early days of our relationship, cheekily claiming he wanted to be able to always have my scent with him. A slow, creeping unease spreads through my body.

Then it hits me like a punch. Hayley wasn't at Justin's funeral.

She should have been, with all my other friends from work. I realize I haven't heard from her either. Not a single call or text.

Could Justin have been having an affair with Hayley? Is that why she didn't turn up at the funeral? Why I haven't heard a word from her?

The discovery of the scarf twists a new lens on a night we

were all out together just a couple of weeks ago. There were ten of us all told, including Will, Molly, and Hayley. Justin sailed us all past the VIP rope at a pulsing pop-up club set up in an old warehouse downtown. I danced. I drank. It got late. I got tired. I went to look for my husband to have him take me home.

I found him with Hayley. Not *with* her, nothing so obvious. They were only talking. He had one hand planted on the wall against which she leaned. In the flashes of colored strobe lights, I watched as Justin arched in toward her.

They seemed so intimate, their heads tilted toward each other, a strange urgency apparent even though I couldn't hear a word. My breath caught in my throat as I anticipated Justin's next move.

I wanted to rush forward and yank him away. I wanted to stay still and see what he did next. Instead I turned away, went to the bathroom, and threw some cold water on my face.

I felt jealous and angry, but I also knew I was tipsy and tired. So much of Justin's energy was going into Convincer as of late that I was feeling a little neglected. I didn't want to overreact.

Justin found me just as I emerged from the restroom. He proposed we call it a night and I agreed. I couldn't wait to get away from the club, but stepping out of the noise and the heat into the cool and quiet night, I felt vulnerable and exposed.

We stood in silence as we waited for a valet to bring Justin's car around.

It took forever. Justin got irritated, muttering under his breath, popping his neck. I could see the rage building in him. I'd only seen it surface twice before, but that was enough to know I didn't want it anywhere near me again. The echoes of slamming doors and shattered glass still ricocheted in my head.

That was the very first time that I thought: *This was a mistake. This whole marriage was a mistake.*

The thought thrilled me and terrified me. I shoved it away. It felt like a betrayal. Of Justin. Of myself. Of our solemn vows.

Finally, a valet handed over Justin's car. He tipped well (Justin always did) but delivered a venomous insult in Greek along with a beatific smile. The valet was oblivious, but I wasn't; Justin had explained the vile expression to me the first time I heard him use it. It involves sheep assholes; no one needs to know any more. My lips tightened. I crossed my arms over my chest.

"What?" Justin drawled as we merged into traffic. "Why so quiet?"

"I think you know."

"The Greek? Come on, Annie. I was blowing off a little steam. The guy had no idea. Anyway, better that I say it in Greek than in English. Or Spanglish."

"You're being a dick."

"Lighten up." Justin gave my knee a quick squeeze and flashed me his brilliant smile, before turning his gaze back to the road.

I felt belittled. I went cold and still. I was furious.

I wished I'd drunk a little less.

"I needed that! Fucking great night, wasn't it?" Justin queried. "That DJ was lit."

"Yeah. Lit."

"What's up, Annie O? Are you mad about that valet? You can't blame a guy for wanting to get his wife home quickly after a night out. Particularly when she looks this hot." His hand slid up my leg and I pushed it away.

I bit my tongue. Until I couldn't. "If I look so fucking 'hot,' what were you doing with Hayley Hayter?"

"What are you talking about?"

"I *saw* you," I stressed, irritated with the games.

"Honestly, Annie, I don't know what you're talking about. I hardly even *saw* Hayley all night except to say hello and good-bye." The look he gave me was pure injured innocence.

"I saw you together! For god's sake, Justin, just tell me the truth."

"I don't know what you think you saw, but you're mistaken. Why would I be interested in Hayley when I have you?" Justin flashed me the smile that had melted my heart so many times before.

I wanted desperately to believe him. But if that was the case, what had I seen? Had my jealous imagination taken a casual farewell and twisted it?

Justin turned the conversation then, animatedly telling me about an admittedly funny encounter he and Will had with a couple of Will's former colleagues that I had only been able to observe, and not hear, in the noise of the club. He wound up to the punch line, delivered it. I gave a begrudging laugh.

His simmering anger had melted away. I didn't want to bring it back to the surface. It was late. I was tired. I wanted my husband to take me home. I swallowed the bitter pill of my jealousy, anger, and fear, and let Justin off the hook. I convinced myself it was all in my imagination and I didn't think about it again.

Now I stare at the richly scented scarf twisted between my fingers and the poison pill explodes in my gut.

CHAPTER TWENTY

WILL

When Justin returned from a ski trip to Mammoth head over heels for a girl he'd met, I at first greeted his enthusiasm with good-natured skepticism. After all, Justin possessed the eager excitement of a golden Lab; he was endlessly erupting in enthusiasm over a new idea or a new person he'd met; it was part of his charm.

I soon realized that his feelings for Annie were different. I thought this was a good sign actually. As much as I appreciated Justin's energy, he burned the candle at both ends and I was sometimes afraid he would burn out. In his first few weeks of dating Annie, he seemed calmer and more focused.

Things were cooking at work, with Justin more excited every day about the technological advances the team was putting together. Our small band was humming along to our target launch date. Justin's romance seemed like a logical progression of sorts.

He finally asked me to meet her, after several weeks of what I will admit was ruthless ribbing on my part. Justin seemed unexpectedly nervous, which I found kind of endearing.

And I liked her. More than liked her. Annie aroused something protective in me. I didn't want to compete for her; it wasn't like that. I just wanted to keep her safe. I still do.

That night at Skyspace was crazy fun: the thrill of having a private advance tour of the various exhibits; the exhilaration of flying down that glass tube on the outside of the building; the easy pleasure in finding the three of us striding the pavement at the end of the night, arms linked, a happy trio. I was giddily expectant—thrilled that Justin was so content and sure that this enviable state would flow over to me, as did so much of Justin's spirit.

Now I pound on Annie's front door, frantic. "Let me in, Annie," I shout. "We need to talk."

Finally, she cracks the door open, and I push inside. "Did you notice who wasn't at the funeral?" I press as soon as I've crossed the threshold.

"Hayley Hayter," Annie replies with a bitter edge to her voice.

"What? No." I look at her in confusion. "Warren Sax."

"That's less surprising. He's a notoriously reclusive billionaire and she is one of our best friends. Supposedly."

"I don't know why you're going on about Hayley. Listen to me. Warren Sax has never heard of Justin." Annie stares at me like I'm speaking in tongues. I elaborate. "Never met him. Didn't even know his name."

"What? That's ridiculous. Why would you even say that?"

"I spoke to Sax myself. Your cousin Lizzie got him on the phone for me."

"Oh." Annie crosses her arms over her chest, bracing herself for what's coming next.

"Everything Justin told us about Sax—working for him, his

putting up the seed money for Convincer—none of it is true, according to Sax himself."

"Then who did put the money in?"

"I don't have a fucking clue."

I look into Annie's eyes and only see despair. She's wan and listless and I feel a bit brutish for having dropped this bomb. We stand in silence for a long time. It's only then that I notice Annie's wearing Justin's blazer over nothing more than a black bra. A pair of oversized jeans are secured around her waist by one of his silk ties.

"Do you think Justin killed himself?" Annie finally asks. Raw pain hoarsens her timbre.

"*What?* God. No. I don't know. It was an accident, right? The police said."

Annie challenges me. "Justin was different right before he died. Surely you felt it too. *Absent* in a way? Distracted. I couldn't get through to him. He always seemed somewhere else. And the *Valium*? It's just not like him . . ."

I nod, weighing her words. I'd also sensed Justin was not fully present lately. I thought it was just the pressure of our imminent launch and didn't make too much of it. I was distracted too, focused on managing so many spinning plates I needed a top hat and a magician's assistant.

"And now, this information about Sax? What else don't we know?" Annie demands.

"What are you getting at?" I ask sharply. "Where's all this coming from?"

"I think Justin might have been having an affair with Hayley Hayter," Annie admits, eyes full of pain and shame.

I'm incredulous. "I can't believe that; he was completely committed to you."

Annie shakes her head softly. "I don't know. There are so many unanswered questions. So many things I may never get answers to. It's fucking torture."

I'm afraid to tell her that I'm beginning to suspect the answers to her questions will be far more painful than living with uncertainty. And that I may be compelled to go dig for them all.

CHAPTER TWENTY-ONE

CAROL

My boy went away to college. It felt like I'd snapped my fingers and he was all grown up. The devastation that consumed me was staggering. This is a common sentiment, I'm aware, perhaps particularly acute in single mothers; nonetheless I was unprepared for the gale-force hit.

I'd expected newfound freedom and time, all of which I was going to use to date (rather than prowl), socialize with friends, maybe take a class in something frivolous that interested me.

Instead I found myself inert, barely dragging myself to house showings and the office when necessary and crawling back into bed without bothering to get out of my clothes as soon as I got back home.

Dating seemed like a stupid chore. My handful of genuine friends had lives already firmly enmeshed with people who'd found more time for them in the past. Attempts were made, but I realized belatedly that you get out of friendships what you've invested. Many situational friends, moms from Justin's school or his extracurriculars, faded away along with those activities.

I looked at a few websites, considered pottery or Italian lessons, and felt completely pathetic.

Desolate emptiness.

I don't know how else to describe it. After years of focus on Justin, on his health, his emotional well-being, his education, his every choice and opportunity, he was existing out in the world without me. It felt like my very beating heart was stripped bare of the protection of skin and muscle and rib cage, exposed and vulnerable to all of life's evils.

Sleeping took up an inordinate amount of my time. I'd perk up when Justin called full of excitement about his classes, his new friends and experiences. I swore I'd never let him know how I was suffering. I wanted him to fully embrace every opportunity that came his way.

My "phone fake" became honed. I would sound cheerful and completely on the ball in conversation, only to click off and slink back into the pillows and the black hole of my despair.

When it was finally Parents' Weekend, I drove to Justin's school vibrating with anticipation. It was the first time in weeks I'd bothered with my appearance, even managing a visit to the salon the day before for a haircut and color. The drive was pleasant enough. It was a crisp, clear day and as I headed north I was treated to trees flaming with a rich array of autumn colors.

The campus was bright with welcoming banners. I found a place to park and walked over to meet Justin at his dorm as we had arranged. There was a spring in my step and I could feel the smile already forming on my lips.

I remembered dropping him off here the last week of August. How I stood watching him from under the shadow of an oak tree as he barreled off into his new life without even a backward glance at me.

"Wait up!" he'd called to a group of young men, and they parted to include him and swallowed him up. I watched them until I couldn't pick out which one of the bobbing heads was his.

Completely lost in my thoughts, I collided head-on with a tall man carrying a bouquet of flowers. I apologized, and took him in as I did: gray hair, lots of it; strong eyebrows and amused eyes.

"Quite all right," he assured me. "No harm done. Tell me the truth," he continued, gesturing with the bouquet. "Are these as ugly as I think? They were all I could find in town, but I suspect my daughter might prefer me empty-handed."

The flowers were indeed sad and sorry, blue spray-painted carnations several days past their sell date. His woebegone expression made me laugh.

"I'm sure you can make up for it with a good meal somewhere. From what I've heard from my son, the dining hall food is not great."

"Is your son a freshman?" the man asked.

"Yes. Your daughter?"

He nodded. "Hasn't been easy. Her mom died when she was seven and it's been just the two of us ever since. It's the longest we've ever been apart and I'm a nervous wreck."

I was completely charmed. How could I not be? Our experiences were so similar and he was so sweetly open about his struggle that it made me feel a little less overwhelmed by my own. "I'm an only parent too," I offered. "Since my son was ten. I totally get it."

I advised him to ditch the carnations and he tossed them

away with a rueful grin. We walked toward the dorms together and discovered we both had dinner reservations at a local seafood restaurant, rated one of the best in the area.

Justin was in front of me then, rushing into my embrace with unabashed need. As my arms circled him and I inhaled his familiar scent, everything else disappeared.

Justin took me to a sample freshman seminar. We toured the new sports complex. Nibbled the "tastes of Connecticut" offerings presented in a series of booths on the quad. We happened to run into Justin's favorite professor, a forthright woman teaching a required economic theory class, who, as he said, "had lit up his brain."

Later, as the two of us dissected what we had gotten out of the sample seminar on myth and archetype, I felt my own brain awaken. The idea of a class of my own didn't seem impossible or far-fetched now, but positively brilliant.

We arrived at the seafood restaurant five minutes before our reservation. My tall friend who'd abandoned his carnations that morning stood in the vestibule with a girl unmistakably marked as his daughter by her height and full dark eyebrows.

He and I nodded amiably at each other. "Good day?" I asked.

"The best," he answered. "This is my daughter, Daisy. And I'm Aaron. Aaron Roth. I don't think we introduced ourselves before."

"Carol Childs," I announced, extending my hand. "This is my son, Justin. Do you two kids know each other? You're both freshmen."

"Everyone knows Justin." Daisy smiled at him. "He's, like, already *campus famous*."

"Campus famous?" Aaron questioned with a wry tilt of his head. "Uh-oh, that sounds dangerous."

"That's why we're sworn to secrecy, shhh." Daisy put her index finger up to her lips and *winked* at Justin.

I have to admit I was amused. What hijinks had my darling boy gotten up to that had made him *campus famous*? His bashful, pleased expression made something shift in me. I realized I didn't want to know.

With sudden blinding clarity I recognized that Justin had to be free to grow away from me, and with that realization I felt freer too. I found myself standing a little straighter, rolling my shoulders back and raising my head. When I did, I was looking directly into Aaron's eyes.

He was looking at me the way a man looks at a woman if you get my meaning.

"I was hoping to see you again," he said softly.

Before I could reply, the hostess proclaimed our table ready. Justin announced he was *starving,* with great dramatic flair. I followed him to our table, but paused to hand Aaron one of my business cards before I did.

Justin and I thoroughly enjoyed our meal, cracking into Maine lobsters and splurging with warm apple pie à la mode. I saw Aaron and Daisy leave while we were still lingering over coffee. Aaron gave me a little wave, which made me feel hopeful.

I drove Justin back to his dorm, with promises of all of his favorite dishes when he came home for Thanksgiving. I piloted back to Long Island with a renewed sense of spirit.

For the next few days, an anticipatory thrill coursed through me every time my phone rang. I not only hoped Aaron would call, I *expected* as much. As time went on, and I didn't hear from him, I shrugged off the sting with a series of rationalizations: He had lost my card; he was busy; he decided it would be awkward for the kids if it didn't work out for us.

Reminding myself it had been a mere chance encounter and no more, I resolved to put Aaron out of my thoughts. I joined a book club and signed up for a Mediterranean cooking class. The teacher was a gorgeous Greek guy named George, and he and I became a thing for several months.

Thinking about George makes me sigh. He was fun. And sweet. But Justin came home for the summer and I became locked in my son's orbit once again. I apologized to George and meant it, as I broke dates or ignored his needs, but when I looked up at the end of the summer he was gone.

I'm back in my Wilshire Corridor apartment now, watching condolence flowers wilt onto the dining room table crowded with bouquets.

Why *do* people send flowers when someone dies? They decay so fast, sickly sweet in scent, brilliant colors quickly gone smudged and brown. We should send cacti, with their hostile spines and minimal need for water; they seem a far more fitting emblem of the need for resilience in the face of death.

My apartment is no more empty than usual; I've lived here alone since I moved to L.A., but today it feels especially still and quiet. Perhaps it's simply the contrast to the fervor of the funeral and the tumult of the bar afterward. More likely it's the overwhelming recognition of just how empty my life is now.

There never will be grandchildren spilling across my threshold as I had imagined. I'll never be the happy babysitter urging Justin and Annie to go out for date nights and away for vacations, all of us secure with me taking charge of their little ones.

Forward, there is nothing; my family line is ended. I can only look back. Death upon death, loss upon loss has been visited on me and all I have now are my memories. The fondest of them are, of course, about Justin, my golden child and my most recent and most savage grief.

Campus famous. He was more than that. He was doing great things. He was a great man. The world has lost one of its exceptional men and I pledge to devote the rest of my life to preserving and protecting Justin's legacy.

It's the least I can do. What any mother would.

CHAPTER TWENTY-TWO

ANNIE

Will snores softly on the sofa. We talked for hours last night, dancing around questions and fears more than confronting them directly. The amount of alcohol we consumed didn't help. Finally, I handed him a pillow and a blanket and directed him to go to sleep. He was in no state to drive and we have a plan (of sorts) for today.

This morning, in the cold, hungover light of day, I have to admit that I'd patched and papered over more than one thing that seemed incongruent, if not outright weird, in order to preserve the picture of Justin I'd created in my head.

Probably the most egregious behavior I ultimately chose to ignore occurred about five months into our perfect romance when Justin ghosted me for three full weeks. I texted him several times. First an ordinary *heya*; then an *are you okay?* punctuated with a smiley face. Finally, a simple *call me?* He didn't.

I left one voicemail message expressing concern. Then backed off.

I was in agony. I tortured myself by cycling through various scenarios: He'd tired of me, fallen for someone else; he was comatose in the hospital after a tragic hit and run; he was too much of a coward to break up with me in person; he had been abducted by aliens. (I knew that last option was ludicrous but I was desperate.)

I thought about calling or texting Will, but I *would not* be a girl who chased after a man who'd made it clear he wasn't interested. I was confused and wounded, but I had my pride. Bella, Felicia, and a few other solid friends rallied around, taking me out for drinks and letting me rant.

Bella ranted back when Justin went quiet on me. A lot. Alternating between two main themes: *I always suspected something, he was too good to be true* and *You deserve a man who will treat you right.*

While I, of course, agreed with the latter, my love-wrenched heart rejected the former. I didn't want to believe I had been dumped or duped. I knew in my *bones* what we had together. I missed Justin desperately, but as the days dragged on, I gradually battened down my urge to talk about him and resolved to move on.

I didn't hear from Will either, a double blow. I'd lost Justin, but JAWs was also no more. The tribe had disbanded. Or at least had abandoned me.

By day 18, a cold kernel of anger had taken root. *How dare he disappear on me? Who the fuck did he think he was? Who did they both think they were?*

An ugly, critical voice screamed back: *Of course he ditched you. He's Justin Childs. He's magic. What are you? Dull, failed, ordinary, nothing.*

nothing [ˈnə-thiŋ]

  noun, 1. no thing, not anything; 2. no part, no portion; 3. one of no consequence, significance, or interest

A therapist told me once that if I heard a parent speaking to a child the way I speak to myself, I'd call the Department of Children and Family Services. That gave me some perspective, but old habits die hard.

I imagined Justin on an island with a supermodel; I thought I saw him one night at the Farmers Market. I wore his hoodie to bed every night (which I didn't dare confess to Bella). Most of those nights I cried myself to sleep.

Day 22 was a Sunday. I'd begged off offers of brunch or a flea market ramble. I planned a day alone in front of the television. My sole goal for the day was to stay in my pajamas.

I'd laid in everything I might need the night before: fizzy water, fruit, chocolate, bagels for breakfast, a pre-cooked chicken to gnaw whenever, trail mix and tortilla chips for snacking. *It's good to have options.*

I slept until a luxurious 9:42. Splashed water on my face, peed, and took a hot cup of coffee rich with half-and-half back into bed. First up, I'd planned *All About Eve,* and I pressed PLAY snuggling comfortably against my headboard. Cinnamon Toast curled into a ball on my stomach and purred contentedly.

At least somebody loves me.

The wonderful few months I'd had with Justin had begun to jumble into a kind of murky swamp. I'd parsed past events and built a case against him, minor slights tabulated, tiny failures mirrored large in memory. My wounded heart was not so much healing as hardening.

Wanting to stay in the black-and-white realm, I watched *The Maltese Falcon* next. These films seemed of a simpler time, for all of the heartache and betrayal on display.

Sydney Greenstreet was in the midst of his furious temper tantrum over the revelation that the Falcon was in fact a fake, when I heard a *click*.

It was the distinct sound of a key in my front door lock. Bella had a key, as did my mother and the building super, but none of them usually dropped by without letting me know in advance. *Would they?* Bella had been worried about me and I'd been avoiding my mother.

I wasn't scared. It was broad daylight. I lived in a building in which my neighbors and I heard one another whether we wanted to or not. It was someone with a key.

Bella, I decided, determined to drag me out.

Equally resolute to resist all such efforts, I drew the blankets up around my neck, grabbed a handful of tissues, and produced three pretty impressive fake sneezes. Cinnamon Toast leapt from my lap indignantly.

The roses arrived in the room before the person carrying them. There were so many blood-red blooms that they barely made it through the doorway. When Justin emerged as their carrier, a barrage of thoughts flooded my brain:

I wish I had brushed my teeth. Thank god he's all right. This had better be fucking good. I won't be bought with flowers. Goddamn him, I was just getting to the other side!

Justin deposited the huge bouquet on my dresser, obscuring the film playing on the TV above it. I pressed PAUSE on the remote. Made a promise to myself to let him speak, but also one to remember my *worth*. My insides were flopping like a freshly beached fish.

"Annie, I owe you an apology," Justin began.

Damn right you do. I pressed my lips together in a thin line. *Just listen. But guard your heart.*

"Something happened and I didn't know how to talk to you about it. So I did the cowardly thing and stopped talking to you completely."

I was bursting with questions. And anger. And excitement. And also a sense of *rightness;* I hadn't been crazy, after all. This man, this relationship had been *real.*

Justin settled himself a careful distance from me on the bed. Close enough to touch, but not touching.

"I was getting these headaches, really knocked me down and out. I didn't tell you because I didn't want to worry you. But they wouldn't stop, so I went to a neurologist." He looked pointedly at me and held my gaze. "She told me I had a brain tumor."

A gasp escaped me. I instinctively leaned forward and grasped his hand. Justin sat rigidly. Cracked his neck to each side. *Pop! Pop!*

"I couldn't ask you to stay with me through that kind of ordeal," he continued. "We haven't known each other long enough. It didn't seem fair. Will argued with me, it might interest you to know; he thinks I've been a dick."

"Will is right," I managed to choke out, for which I was rewarded with one of Justin's glorious smiles.

"But here's the thing, it turns out the neuro was wrong! Three other doctors later and it seems I'm fine. Well, maybe a terrible boyfriend, but I'm not going to die of brain cancer. At least not this week, anyway. I'm so sorry, Annie."

"How could you think I would . . . ? Don't you know I would stand by you through anything?"

"You would, wouldn't you?" Justin's eyes were serious, blazing into mine with a love so fierce I had to avert my gaze.

He tilted my face back to his. "You know that I've lost a lot of people. I couldn't bear the thought of losing you too, so I did the really mature thing and ran away first. I have no excuse, I'm an ass."

"I hate you," I murmured in a tone laden with love. "Really, really hate you."

He rained kisses on every inch of my body, while crooning endearments: *You're so beautiful; I'm so sorry; I'll never do something like that again; I was just so scared; I love you; I can't live without you. Please don't be mad.*

My body unfolded like petals in spring sunshine.

He fucked me then, unbrushed teeth and all.

At first, Bella was loud in my ear with her opinions: *You don't disappear on someone you love, no matter what the reason. He's a runner, Annie. He'll run again.*

I didn't want to hear it and so I didn't. I'd shut Bella down so hard her teeth rattled. It was the first real rift we've had since we were seated next to each other in fourth grade. Our friendship survived middle school, high school, and attending college across the country from each other, and it had only been further cemented when we were both back in L.A. But her unveiled condemnation of Justin nearly broke us apart.

After Justin and I were engaged, Bella kept her mouth shut, but I sensed her unease around him.

I chalked it up to jealousy—not sexual, but it was certainly true that Justin had displaced Bella as my main confidant and partner in crime.

Our wedding itself was epic. Justin would have never settled for anything less.

My dress turned out magnificently, after all. It was a risqué choice for me, but not for Mrs. Justin Childs, and as I walked down the aisle in daringly cut tulle and silk to greet him, I remember thinking that the dress was like my chrysalis. After the wedding I would blossom into my new role. *Annie Elizabeth Hendrix Childs.*

It was a beautiful, sunny Los Angeles afternoon. We gathered 225 of our nearest and dearest onto a tented expanse of lawn at the Hotel Bel-Air for a sweet and emotional ceremony. Justin and I both welled up when we exchanged our rings and Bella was handy with lace-trimmed hankies.

The party afterward was a rager for the ages. Justin hired a sixteen-piece band with a heavy brass section as well as whimsically attired performers who roved among the guests throughout the night, surprising them with fanciful little gifts like puzzles, balloon animals, and crystal ball readings. Fire dancers closed the night, dazzling with their fiery torches and athletic moves.

I pick up a framed photo from our wedding day. Justin's seated. I'm perched on his lap. His arms circle my waist and while my face is angled more toward Justin than toward the camera, you can still see I am gazing at him with unbridled adoration. It's how I felt that day. Like an already lucky girl who was now *the luckiest girl in the world.*

I need to think. I need to sort the jumble of information ricocheting around my brain. Okay. What do I know? Know for *certain*?

My husband was a liar. That much is true.

I decide to start a list of known facts and questions about my husband.

1. Justin Childs, age 33, deceased.

When *was* the first time I felt even *a hint* that things were not as they seemed? I cast my mind back, parsing our relationship under the sudden, harsh light of doubt.

Was there any clue *before* Justin ghosted me because of his misdiagnosis? With a sudden lurch of my stomach I realize I don't know if Justin *ever really had* that brain tumor scare. I took it at face value, even respecting his desire not to talk about it after, but what if it was bullshit? What if that was why he told me never to speak of it?

Then again, *why would anyone make up such a horrific thing?*

I need coffee. I make a pot and while it brews, I gulp a glass of cold water and a couple of aspirins. I feed Cinnamon Toast and give her fresh water. Our kitchen is charming, one of the projects we'd managed to (almost) complete. The walls are a sunny yellow; the '50s retro Formica table has matching yellow boomerangs and the metal chairs yellow vinyl seats. This particular morning, I find all this cheeriness oppressive.

When the coffee's ready I pour two cups and walk over to Will's prone form. Setting the cups down on the low-slung table in front of the sofa, I give his shoulder a soft shake.

"Will," I urge. "Get up."

He grunts and burrows his head deeper into a pillow.

"Will. What did Justin tell you about his brain tumor?"

Will rolls over and rubs sleep from his eyes. "His what?"

"Remember, he and I had only been going out a few months when he got the misdiagnosis? He disappeared on me for like three weeks and . . ." I trail off, realizing that Will is looking at me like I'm completely crazy. My voice is shrill as I continue. "He *told me* you said he was a dick to keep it from me!"

Pushing himself up to a sitting position, Will lifts a steaming mug to his mouth and sips. "Well, it's what I would have said if I knew he'd done such a thing, but"—he shrugs—"I don't know what you're talking about."

FACTS ABOUT MY HUSBAND

1. Justin Childs, age 33, deceased
2. Medical history: uncertain
3. Pathological liar: quite certain

I drain half of my own cup. The liquid is scalding, but I barely feel it. "Do you think it's possible he hid it from you?"

Will's eyes are bleak. "I don't know. It's possible, I guess."

We spend the next few minutes looking at a calendar and pinpointing the exact three weeks that Justin had gone AWOL on me. It wasn't all that difficult; I'd practically carved the dates into my flesh.

"We were up north together then," Will affirms. "For a fund-raising trip. Not the entire three weeks, but two of them. Then Justin came back to L.A. and I went to see my mother for a couple of days. If something was going on with him medically then, it's news to me."

"Why on earth would Justin tell me he had been diagnosed with *a brain tumor*?"

Out loud the question seems even more ludicrous than when it was just banging around in my head. "I was already so in love with him, I would have forgiven him anything when he came back!"

"Would you have, though? Think about it, Annie, if Justin had turned up after three weeks of no contact with some lame-ass excuse, would you really have welcomed him back with open arms?"

I want to protest, but I fall silent. Cinnamon Toast stalks into the room, and twines around my legs as if sensing my distress.

As mad as I was for Justin, Bella's words of caution would have certainly resonated more soundly if not for his *bravery* at keeping the *terrible news* to himself *in order to spare me.*

"I loved him so much." The words escape my lips in a whisper.

"I know. I did too," Will replies gently. "That's what makes it so awful. But we could both be up to our necks in the mess Justin left behind. So we better stop grieving and figure some shit out."

FACTS ABOUT MY HUSBAND

1. Justin Childs, age 33, deceased
2. Medical history: uncertain
3. Pathological liar: quite certain
4. Truly mourned

Does that sound crazy? The depth to which we both still love Justin? It must. I'm beginning to suspect that our relationship was one of lies of commission and omission, the depth and breadth of which I'm only beginning to untangle.

"Where do we even begin?" The question bursts out of me.

"Do you still want to confront Hayley?" Last night's burning energy to *do something* seems considerably more daunting in the light of day, but I need answers.

"I do."

I can't help but think of our wedding vows, mine and Justin's, handcrafted and sprinkled with a chorus of "I do!"s as punctuation to each asked promise.

Do you promise to love, adore, and court me forever?

I do!

Do you promise to be faithful to me and attentive to my desires?

I do!

Do you promise to not die in a car wreck, leaving me stunned and destroyed?

We didn't actually include that one. But maybe we should have.

CHAPTER TWENTY-THREE

WILL

I've never been to Hayley Hayter's house. Pulling up to the modest stucco Spanish-style cottage in an enclave of Culver City known as Sunkist Park, I'm struck not by the house so much, or the profusion of hot pink bougainvillea that drapes it, but by the many MISSING posters that paper the house's front archway. A picture of Hayley smiles from the poster's center, a curly-haired girl with soft features and the slightly bucktoothed grin caught in this photograph.

Four people wearing T-shirts emblazoned with the same image are assembled on the front patio, opening boxes of even more flyers.

I glance over at Annie, who looks pale as a ghost. A lump of dread forms in the pit of my stomach.

"Hayley's *missing*?" Annie rasps.

"Apparently," I reply grimly.

We exit the car and walk up the flower-lined path in front of the house. A soft breeze leavens the burgeoning heat of the day.

I catch sight of a soft-featured face surrounded by a mop of curly brown hair and my heart leaps. For a brief moment I think it is Hayley herself, safe and sound. Then my eyes focus on the lines of the neck and jaw and I realize I'm looking at a male version of Hayley's features. Upon catching sight of us, he strides toward us with an aggressive swagger.

Annie sees him barreling toward us. "We're stuck now," she murmurs to me.

"Hello," she says to the curly haired man. "You're Hugh, right? Hayley's brother? I'm Annie Childs? I worked, uh, work with Hayley? This is my friend Will Barber."

Hugh's soft features harden. "So you're the famous Annie." His voice drips with venom. I can see a pulse flutter in the hollow of Annie's throat. "Here to help?" he continues snidely. "I would think you've done enough."

"Hey!" I interject. "I don't know what you think you're talking about, but Annie is Hayley's friend. And she just lost her own husband. Show a little respect."

"What's going on anyway?" Annie asks. "What's happened to Hayley?"

"Hayley's gone missing. Hasn't been seen for four days."

"God. I'm so sorry," Annie blurts.

"A little too late for that, isn't it? I know all about your husband," Hugh sneers. "Kept Hayley on the hook for months while he agonized about his precious vows. That motherfucker wanted Hayley and she wanted him, but he never went all the way downtown if you get my drift."

It occurs to me Hugh might be on something. Annie's gone even paler, stricken by his crude words. "Look," I assert. "There's no reason to be a dick."

"There's every reason," Hugh spits back. "Her husband was

jerking my sister around for months. Then Hayley goes missing and he turns up dead? Don't tell me there's no connection. I don't know what he did to her or what he got her involved in, but you are not welcome here. Do you know that the cops interrogated *me*? For ten goddamn hours! Now get the fuck off our property."

The trio on the patio is staring at us now, beginning to mass protectively behind Hugh. One of them must be Hugh's mother. Her exhausted face creases in distress as she reaches a protective hand toward her son.

"Let's go, Will," Annie whispers. "Now." We turn our backs on Hugh's ugly leer and hurry back to my car.

"You see why I don't know what to think? What to believe?" Annie's voice is shrill as we pull away. "Hayley's brother confirmed there was something going on between them!"

"But that they weren't sleeping together."

"So what? An emotional affair is almost worse. It *is* worse. How could I be so stupid? And Hayley's missing? What the fuck is going on?"

I take a deep breath, about to put voice to something that I've hardly dared to think. "I don't believe he was having an affair with Hayley, but he might have been using her."

"For what?" The tremor in Annie's voice betrays the intensity of her emotions.

"I don't know exactly. It just fits his pattern."

"His pattern?" Annie's eyebrows arch up.

"It was a thing Justin would do," I say carefully. "Even way back in B school. Turn on that love light. Make people think he wanted to sleep with them, be with them. Dangle it. In return they gave him anything he asked."

"But what could he have wanted from Hayley?"

"I'm not sure."

We drive in silence as I steel myself for what I know I must do next.

"Okay. Here goes," I say finally. "I'll call Sunil. As much as I'm dreading this conversation."

"Are you going to tell him about Sax?" Annie asks anxiously.

"Not yet. Not outright. Too many people are depending on me. I need to figure out what the hell is going on first."

I dial Sunil, but the call goes to voicemail. Part of me is relieved, even though I know I'm just delaying the inevitable. I leave a message asking him to call me as soon as possible.

"We should eat," I say.

"Whatever." Annie shrugs. "I'm not hungry."

"You should still eat. Let's go to Rae's."

Annie nods.

To fill the space between us, I flick on the radio. It jolts a ska punk riff into the car; an angry singer growls a raspy refrain of "No, not now, not ever," on repeat. Annie reaches over and turns the radio off. Silence descends again.

Annie finally breaks it. "Wherever this is headed, it's going to be bad, isn't it?"

I can feel Annie's eyes on me, but I keep my own eyes steadfastly on the road in front of me and my mouth shut. She's right. This is headed nowhere good at all.

"You know all the palm trees in L.A. are dying, right? They're not native to the city. So they're all going to die and there are no plans to replace them. In a couple of years, the whole city'll look different."

"They'll have to reprint all the postcards," I reply.

"Yeah. Maybe we could come up with an idea for *Shark*

Tank," Annie zings back. "A Postcard Palm Tree Removal System."

I glance at Annie and see a quick flash of smile cross her lips. Surprised by the turn in the conversation, I hesitate, and Annie bursts into laughter. It's full and rich and shakes her entire body. She clutches her sides, gasping for breath. There's a touch of hysteria to it, and I just let her run her course without comment.

Finally, she wipes her eyes and takes a deep shuddering breath. "I know nothing's funny," she affirms with a shrug. "But if I don't laugh . . ." For a second she looks like she might cry.

I take her hand and give it a quick squeeze. "No worries. You do you."

"Thank you. I don't know how I'd get through all this without you."

"JAWs forever," I pledge, only to sense her quick recoil. "Hey, no matter what we learn about Justin, I know he loved us both."

"In his fashion."

"What do you mean?"

"Come on, Will. He may have loved us, but what does that amount to if he lied to us about *everything*? Warren Sax! Brain tumors! Affairs! God knows what else. Has it occurred to you that his brother, Tommy, might be another figment of Justin's imagination?"

"That's . . ." I trail off, my protest frozen in my throat. Could Justin have created a fictional addicted, suicidal brother all those years ago? It suddenly seems possible. I have to acknowledge that everything I took for granted must now be tested. And what proof did I have that Tommy ever existed?

"You may be right," I agree. "We need to question everything. But more than that, we need to be prepared for wherever the answers take us."

Another slightly unhinged giggle escapes Annie. "No promises."

Annie's phone buzzes. She glances at the screen. "Oh my god," she says. "It's Carol. I can't answer it. I just can't talk to her right now." Annie hits DECLINE.

"We could just ask her about Tommy point-blank," I hazard.

"Here's the thing, though, Will. I mentioned Tommy to Carol at the funeral and she looked at me like I was crazy. And Justin told me to never talk about him with her so I just never did, before yesterday, I mean. Seems suspicious now, doesn't it?"

"He asked me to do the same. I didn't think anything about it at the time except that he was being protective of Carol, like always."

"Right."

With sudden, penetrating doubt, I rethink everything I know about Justin's brother and his addiction. We were in our first year of business school when Justin looked at a text on his phone one day and went pale. He hurriedly excused himself from the coffee shop we were in, throwing a twenty on the table for his turkey on sourdough.

I didn't see him for five days, despite texting to check in.

He finally showed up at my door just as I was darting out for our nine o'clock class. I took a hard look into his eyes. They were red-rimmed. Hesitantly, he laid it out for me: He had a brother back in New York who had overdosed.

"He's alive," Justin continued. "My mom found him in time

and they Narcaned him. But they don't know if it was an accident, or you know, an attempt at suicide."

"Shit. Did you go back to New York?"

He looked at me strangely. "Why would you ask that?"

I got flustered. I'm not sure why, but thinking about it now I
wonder if there was something accusatory in his tone. He went
on to say he just needed some time to get his head together.
"It's not like I can just drop everything and run back to New
York because he fucked up." His tone was angry; his brow
creased.

"Yeah, of course." Suddenly I was rushing to reassure him.
"Sorry. I didn't mean anything."

As the semester went on, he had the occasional unexplained
disappearance. He'd reappear after a few days, mutter something about his brother, but not offer up much in the way of
details. Upon his return, he always seemed haunted, like his
very life force had been sucked, so I did my best to buoy him
along. I shared my notes and essentially carried him on my
back through midterms, drilling him with the flash cards I'd
made for myself. He was always so generous with me, buying
meals, sharing his designer haul; I was happy to repay his generosity any way I could.

The morning of our financial accounting final, a frantic
pounding on my front door woke me from a deep sleep. With
bleary eyes, I checked the time: 4:37 A.M. *Shit.*

Justin was at my door, suitcase in hand.

"What's up, man? You going someplace? Facing the final
can't be that bad."

"Actually, I have to miss it. Tommy finally got it right. I'm on
an eight A.M. flight to New York."

My sleep-fogged brain took a minute to process what Justin

meant by Tommy "got it right." He'd killed himself. Or ODed, which was tantamount to the same thing.

"I'm so sorry," I said and hesitated. Anything else seemed inadequate.

"Yeah. The stupid idiot. Anyway, I'll email the school, but I'm out. My mother needs me at home." He gave me a pained smile and gripped me in a tight, fast hug. "Didn't want you worrying about me, buddy," he said as he released me. "Hopefully, I'll get some kind of accommodation on the finals and I'll be back in January."

I didn't see or hear from Justin again for almost four years. Until he showed up in my office one day and made April Riley giggle.

My head spins as I look at this piece of my history with Justin with brutal new perspective.

The silence between us grows stickier as my thoughts spiral. My brain frantically sorts and categorizes every fact I know about Justin, my best friend and business partner, looking for holes and inconsistencies. There was so much I accepted, just because Justin told me so.

This time it's Annie who flicks the radio on, filling the car with a pulsing beat and screeching vocals. It's angry music, edgy and defiant. We keep the volume up high.

CHAPTER TWENTY-FOUR

CAROL

Annie doesn't pick up. I'm not surprised; I didn't actually expect she would.

I'd dialed Justin's cellphone number at least half a dozen times just to hear his voice before trying her. Overwhelmed by the futility of hearing his same cheerful recorded refrain, "Leave a message and I'll hit you back," over and over again, I called Annie. I leave her a voicemail, asking how she's doing and if she'd like to have a meal one day this week. Low key. No pressure. Kind.

Then I throw the phone across the room and watch with satisfaction as it smacks into the wall and clatters to the floor, the screen shattered. That felt good.

I barely slept last night, despite the two Ambien I gobbled down. Restless, I sweated right through two sets of pajamas and had to strip the still damp sheets as soon as I pulled my ragged body from the bed shortly before dawn. My infrequent dips into slumber were punctuated by fragments of terrifying dreams: images of looming strangers, car crashes, and, of course, fire, all underscored by a pervasive sense of uneasy longing and desperate failure.

After I remade the bed, I showered, dressed, and had a cup of tea and a slice of whole grain toast with my favorite orange marmalade. It was five forty-five in the morning and I had absolutely nothing with which to fill the rest of my day.

I curled in the sofa opposite the window in my living room for quite some time, watching the sun creep across the geometrically patterned area rug that dominates the space. I never would have expected to find myself in California, alone in this starkly modern apartment, in this city that never really feels like a city.

I remember the day Justin first told me he was moving to California. He'd been out of college for about eighteen months, living at home, but hardly ever there. He was following in my footsteps, selling real estate, although he was working for a slick Manhattan outfit that sold commercial buildings as opposed to the middle-class Long Island homes that had been my stock-in-trade.

While I was, of course, happy to have him back home, it was also an adjustment. He was a man, a college graduate and a working professional, and at the same time every time I looked at him I saw the baby in diapers, the toddler grinning, the serious little boy, the gregarious young adolescent.

And while I knew Justin, of course, I also didn't know him at all.

Where he spent most of his nights, who his friends were, if he was dating, these were all mysteries. He breezed in and out of the house without warning, sometimes making me jump when I discovered him inside, sometimes disappearing so soundlessly that I wandered around our place convinced he'd be around the next corner, only to discover it was empty.

I hadn't been *happy* exactly while Justin had been away at school, but I'd found a peaceful rhythm to my existence. I also had the comforting schedule of school breaks and summers; every visit home was defined by his eventual return to college. I found this new order unsettling, which in turn unleashed waves of guilt. Shouldn't I be thrilled without reservation to have my boy at home?

But I did my best. What any mother would do. I tried to ask minimal questions. Gave him his space. I'd periodically announce I was going on a "cultural weekend with friends," and I'd book a room at one of my old haunts in the city. Spend the days wandering solo, the nights in the arms of a stranger.

During one of those weekends, on a brisk and breezy Saturday, two vaguely familiar profiles caught at the corner of my eye as I turned in to the Columbus Circle entrance to Central Park. It was their height, the dark slashes of their eyebrows. The man's eyes met mine and he smiled, an open, genuine smile that I felt down to my core.

"Carol, right?" the tall man inquired. "Aaron and Daisy Roth. Remember, we met the kids' freshman year? I'm so glad to see you looking so well!"

He seemed genuinely astonished that I should look good. I felt myself blush. My eyes slid away from him to find Daisy eyeing me with an expression of sympathetic curiosity. Trying to place just where I'd experienced this particular kind of look before, I realized with horror that she was looking at me much like people did when Mike died. Like I was an object of pity.

Confused by both his effusive words and her physical reaction, I could only stammer, "Nice to see you both. What've you been doing since graduation, Daisy?"

"Oh, I'm working for an immigrants' rights organization."

Aaron smiled at his daughter. "Saving the world one day at a time, this one. And your son?"

"Real estate. Like his mama. Just bigger, bolder, better."

"Good for him. Amazing to see your kids grow up to be their own whole adult human beings, isn't it? I'm so glad you got the chance," he added emphatically.

My confusion only mounted, which must have been apparent on my face because Daisy reached out and laid a gentle hand on my arm. "It's all right. Justin told us about the cancer. How brave you were."

"The cancer?"

Now it was the Roths' turn to look confused. "Your diagnosis, freshman year? Right after we met?" Aaron looked embarrassed. Hurried to explain. "I'm sorry if Justin was supposed to keep it quiet, but I lost your card. When I asked Daisy to ask Justin for it, he told us the sad news."

"Not so sad after all, though!" Daisy piped. "You look wonderful. So healthy."

"Thank you. I am. Very nice to see you both. Good luck, Daisy."

Abandoning my plan for a walk in Central Park, I reversed my steps and returned to my hotel room where I placed the DO NOT DISTURB sign on the door. Collapsing onto the unmade bed, my mind spinning, I desperately tried to make sense of the scene that had just unfolded.

Justin had lied to Daisy. Had told her I had cancer. Had indicated I was so sick that Aaron and Daisy were shocked to see

I was *still alive*. Why would he do such a thing? I curled into the fetal position. Was my son wishing me dead? I felt sick.

I lay there for a long time. The light brightened, then deepened, as the hours passed. Even in the shock of this revelation, I recognized that there had been a spark between me and Aaron Roth, even now, all these years later, and with him believing I was virtually back from the dead.

It dawned on me. Justin must have told this lie to keep Aaron from contacting me. Of course that was it! Justin was just starting school, forging his own identity, yes, but still enough of a boy to want his mama to be 100 percent his, if and when he needed her. As this understanding flooded my body, I uncurled and sat up. Of course. He panicked, told a lie, and then had to live with it.

In his first year of school, I'd asked after Daisy once or twice (a backdoor channel to Aaron, of course), feigning a casualness I didn't quite feel, but Justin shrugged and said they didn't really move in the same crowd. I knew Justin to be a straightforward young man for the most part, no more prone to white lies or evasiveness than anyone else. Now I wondered if he'd deliberately avoided her after his impulsive action, embarrassed by his lie.

That night I went to the bar at Nobu and picked up a photographer from Belgium. He was almost twenty years younger than I was, which was kind of a turn-on. But his hands were clammy and his dick a pencil, so I kicked him out and slept alone. After checking out the next day I drove home to Long Island.

I entered quietly and laid my keys down on the hall table. "Justin?" I called. "I'm home."

He came out from the kitchen, wiping his hands on a dishtowel. "Hi. Good weekend? Full of culture? Or is that really just your group's code word for cocktails?" His eyes twinkled as he teased me.

I embraced him fully, taking him by surprise. "Whoa, Mom. What's up? You okay?"

"I'm just always happy to see my boy."

"You want some breakfast? I was just scrambling eggs."

"Sure."

I followed him into the kitchen. Justin cracked two more eggs into a bowl and whipped them into a froth with a fork.

"I ran into a college friend of yours," I threw out casually, taking one of the two seats at the oval kitchen table.

"Oh yeah? Who's that?"

"Daisy Roth. She was with her dad."

Justin's back was to me but his spine stiffened. He cracked his neck. Two precise pops. "How's she doing?"

"Good. Working with an immigration group of some sort."

"She always was kind of a bleeding heart." Justin poured the beaten eggs into a hot pan sizzling with butter. He turned to face me. "Want toast?"

I looked into his eyes. They were clear, untroubled. Was it possible Daisy got the story wrong altogether? But then I remembered Justin's spine going taut, the crisp cracks of his neck. I screwed together my courage to ask the question.

"No, thanks. Listen, sweetheart . . ."

Before I finished my sentence, Justin interrupted. "Mom, look, no way to say this but to say it. I'm moving to L.A. I got accepted into business school. And I'm going." He looked at me defiantly, like he was prepared for a fight.

"Congratulations! Oh my god. Which school? I'm so proud of you. When do you start?"

Confusion crossed Justin's face. "You're not mad?"

"Mad? Why would I be mad?"

"I thought you liked having me home. I'll be three thousand miles away."

"Oh, honey, I love having you here. But you have to live your own life. I totally understand that. Have I ever stopped you from doing what's best for you?"

The eggs began to smoke. Justin turned off the pan. I pulled a bottle of prosecco from the fridge to toast Justin's acceptance. We began to discuss his program, and apartments in L.A., and whether Justin should ship things out to the coast or just buy new there.

We never spoke about the Roths again.

CHAPTER TWENTY-FIVE

ANNIE

"Why do you think Justin married me?" The words slip from my mouth and I regret them instantly. What could Will possibly say that would soothe the roiling well of hurt and insecurity consuming me?

"And don't tell me he loved me," I snap at Will's obvious struggle to come up with the right words. The fact that I know there are no "right words" only makes me angrier that he can't. "As we've already established, love just isn't enough."

"You had him from the moment you met him, I know that much," Will finally offers softly. "And while he flirted and charmed everyone, everywhere, as you well know, he was different about you. From the beginning and until the end. I don't know how to explain it any more than that."

I try to speak. My throat catches. I tightly grip the purse on my lap, my palms becoming moist against the leather.

So Justin was "different about me." The phrase massages my bruised ego, my need to be special to the man I loved wholeheartedly and married. But the Justin that Will describes is a user, a manipulator who used his charm to get what he wanted. *So what did he want from me?*

With sickening realization, I accept that it always felt too good to be true. That Justin Childs, tall, handsome, magnetic, an ambitious entrepreneur, one of this earth's golden boys, wanted *me*, thought I was pretty *enough*, talented *enough*, interesting *enough*. I'd thought I'd blossom under the umbrella of his love, that his magic would rub off and that one day I'd be worthy of him. I thought he saw that *potential* in me, and was patient and loving enough to wait for me to bloom.

Now I just wonder what he wanted. How I was *used*.

Will brakes for a red light. A beautiful fat tabby crosses the street and I remember Birdie Tonks and her "kids."

With a sudden rush, I become unequivocally convinced that Justin had *absolutely nothing* to do with saving Birdie's cats. *That he decided to claim ownership the very moment he heard me mention an anonymous savior.* Yet I had believed him, been delighted at yet another expression of his devotion, even acquiescing to his request to keep quiet about his benevolence.

It consumes me, this revelation. When else in my relationship with Justin was I manipulated like this?

CHAPTER TWENTY-SIX

WILL

When Sunil calls me back, he delivers a bombshell in response to my casual first question. I ask if there was anything that had struck him odd or strange in our financials in the last few weeks and he replies: *"Did you know that Justin bought a boat?"*

No, I most definitely did not.

The vessel is registered to our company, which is another shock.

"Why didn't you say anything to me before?" I ask, not without edge.

"You two talked about everything. I didn't think I needed to." I can almost hear his shrug through the phone. "I guess it does seem a little weird now."

"It didn't seem weird before?" I explode. "We make VR games! Why the fuck would we need a boat?"

"Look, Will, Justin did a lot of crazy things, we both know that. He told me the boat was for entertaining clients."

"When did he buy it?" I snap.

"Just under two weeks ago."

"For how much?"

"Eighty-five K."

"Jesus! Where's it moored?"

"Marina del Rey."

"What kind of boat is it?" I ask, struggling to keep my voice level. I'm seized by something so powerful, the top of my head tingles; I can feel the blood rushing in my veins. I pull over and put the car in park.

I glance over at Annie. She's rigid in her seat.

"What do I know about boats? I know numbers," Sunil says in response to my last question. "What's up, Will?"

"I'm not entirely sure, man," I reply. I owe him some transparency. He's been a friend since business school and I recruited him into the company. I hesitate. "Look, Sunil, we should meet tomorrow morning early, okay? At the office. I'm going to need a deep dive into the books, including the details of Justin's recent expenditures. Please tell me now that there's nothing more outrageous than a goddamn boat."

"That depends on what you mean by outrageous. You know better than anyone how fast and furious things've been flying lately. But why all the questions? You're making me nervous."

I can't fault Sunil. Justin did impulsive, "crazy" things all the time, but there was always a reveal, an upside, something we didn't cotton on to right away, but that Justin saw playing out four steps down the line. As a result, I just let his freak flag fly, we all did. He'd brought us on this magic carpet ride and we trusted him.

Also, we've been moving at the speed of light as we ramped up to our launch. There's no reason Sunil would have thought it was on him to tell me about the boat because Justin told me everything. Or so we both had thought.

"Okay. Look. Everything will be fine. Text me the slip number. I'll see you in the morning."

I hang up the phone, sick with self-disgust. Duped by a liar, I am turning into a liar. I turn to Annie.

"Did you know Justin bought a boat?"

"He didn't even like the water."

"And how do we know that?"

"Because he said so . . ." Annie trails off. "Point taken."

With remote fascination, I realize my hands are trembling.

"Are you okay, Will?" Annie's brow creases with concern.

I'm not okay. The revelation of the boat tipped the scales. I am a patsy, a dupe, an idiot, a goddamn fool. Parents who lied to me my whole life, and a best friend and partner who I now believe lied to me from the day we met until the day he died.

Nothing about this is okay.

CHAPTER TWENTY-SEVEN

CAROL

I take myself out of my rectangle of an apartment and down to Venice Beach. There are many much nicer beach destinations in L.A. I could have gone up to the pale, open sands of Zuma, for example, or splurged on the expensive-but-worth-it parking at Paradise Cove, or marveled at the rocky beauty of Point Dume. Today I crave the seedy, hippie-homeless vibe of Venice.

It reminds me of New York a little, as if a tiny slice of Times Square at its squalid peak is squared up against the Pacific Ocean.

I park my car in an all-day lot and amble over to the boardwalk. It's a hot clear day, the kind of perfect weather for which L.A. is famous, and as I had hoped, it's brought out all of humanity. I'm hoping that being among a crowd will help me feel a little less lonely.

Vendors hawk original "art," palm readings, dream catchers, wind chimes, ceramic pipes, swimsuits, sarongs. Storefronts promote fast and easy medical marijuana cards, an impossibly wide selection of hats, fantasy figures constructed from repurposed auto parts, or T-shirts and shorts emblazoned with rude images and crude slogans.

Pedestrians clog the walkway. All sorts of conveyances are out as well: scooters, skateboards, bicycles, tricycles and unicycles, roller skates and roller blades.

An ancient, barely clothed man pedals by on a Frankensteined portable home constructed from a bicycle, two shopping carts, and a complex arrangement of tarps. His ink-dark skin glistens with sweat; grizzled iron gray hair cascades down his back.

A tubby family of four passes me, slurping on enormous ice cream–stuffed waffle cones. Tourists, I gauge, based on Dad's bulging tummy pack, the teen daughter's sunburn-blistered shoulders, and Mom's tightly clutched "theft-resistant" travel bag. The son, whom I guess to be about eleven, topples his ice cream from its cone. It lands on the hot cement with a splat. Straggling a few feet behind the rest of the family, he scoops it up and plops it right back, lapping away without missing a beat. A short bark of laughter escapes me as he catches me watching him and gives me a victorious smirk.

I leave the boardwalk and go over to the skateboard bowl. These kids are death-defying as they soar into jumps and twists only to smack onto poured concrete if they miss their board on the descent. I watch a gamine-faced girl with a determined jaw fly high, twist in the air, and land *hard*. No helmet. I *hear* her head whack the pavement. She lies still and silent and my heart thumps wildly in my chest.

I cannot bear any more death.

The girl stirs. Another skater, a Latinx boy with no shirt and oversized shorts, leans over to give her a hand up. I turn away, suddenly sickened by this play that could be so dangerous. The frailty of existence has never felt more overwhelming.

I stumble onto the beach proper and sink down onto the sand. The ocean gleams in front of me, frothy white waves lapping at the shore, huge blue swells beyond. I try to calm myself by timing my breaths to the ebb and flow of the water. I try to find a reason to live.

Slowly, gradually, I give myself over to the understanding that there actually might not be one single reason that I *should* continue my existence on this planet. Who would miss me? Who would care? Besides, why do I deserve to live when everyone else in my life has died?

I don't. In fact, my life of loss and sorrow is only what I deserve.

I push myself up to standing and start to walk, relishing the difficulty of propelling my muscles against the sand's resistance. I begin to consider how I might kill myself. Self-immolation? Appropriate but messy. Pills? That seems easy enough. Pills, I decide.

Lost in my own wicked thoughts, I plow right into a man lying on a beach towel, tipping over onto my hands and knees with a sharp "Ow!"

"Are you all right?" he asks with a heavy accent. Not Mexican. South American maybe?

"Clearly not," I mutter more to myself than in reply. I twist to look at the man I stumbled over. "You?"

"I'm fine. But where is a beautiful woman like you headed in such a hurry?"

I take a good look at him. Mid to late forties would be my guess. Fit and proud of it, as evidenced by his form-fitting bathing trunks. Broad facial planes obscured behind large mirrored sunglasses. A ready smile. He tips his sunglasses down and his eyes meet mine.

Electricity courses through my body. I'm wildly attracted to him, suddenly desperate to feel his body on mine.

"Actually," I offer, demurely dropping my eyes. "I think I hurt my ankle."

That's all it takes. He helps me "limp" off the sand. I find out he's staying at a boutique hotel just down the beach. We walk there, his arm around my waist as I limp beside him, my body lingering against his. We order ice for my ankle and margaritas. Two rounds later we're in his room. The sex is raw and messy and urgent. We come at each other ferociously once, rest, and go again.

He falls asleep and I slip out.

It's gone night. The cool air feels wonderful against my heated skin. I keep a wary eye out as I make my way back to my car, which strikes me as ironic. Here I am contemplating suicide and yet primal survival instinct takes over to keep me on the alert for predators.

I *am* still considering the pills. But it's not time yet. I'm not quite ready to die I realize; I still have appetites, after all.

Besides, Will and Annie are sure to be asking questions; perhaps the police still are as well. Before I take my own life, I must be sure that Justin's legacy is protected, that my precious boy is allowed to rest in peace.

CHAPTER TWENTY-EIGHT

ANNIE

The marina looks idyllic. Tethered brightly white boats bob on blue water, the sun glows hot, the air shimmers. I don't know much about boats, but the ones docked here seem designed for weekend pleasure; they're on the smaller side, mostly sailboats, a few motorboats and speedboats. They are graced with an array of tantalizing names: *Witch of the Water, Donna's Daydream, Reel Obsession, Seaducer.*

What did Justin name the boat he bought? My steps lag and I fall behind Will, who charges ahead of me on the dock with long, determined strides.

What do you do when everything you thought you knew is a lie? I can hear my heart beat loudly in my ears as I'm flooded with shame. *You should have known,* a voice inside my head screams. *You did know, you foolish bitch.*

shame [ˈshām]

noun, 1. a disgrace; 2. embarrassment; 3. stigma

This is now the word that consumes me. I close my eyes as the last layer of protective shock evaporates, leaving me vulnerable to hard truth. *My entire marriage was a lie*. But if Justin was using me, had *targeted* me for some reason, I don't have a clue as to why.

I shudder as I remember writhing under him in abandonment; how, desperate to excite him, I donned lingerie that perverted my body, shoes that cost me my balance, how I pushed my own comfort levels aside in order to seem desirable and exciting. I realize with a sudden overwhelming rush that everything I did with Justin was part of my futile attempt to be *enough,* that a sense of inadequacy drove all my choices, along with willful blindness.

With the ugly realization that my relationship with Justin was grounded in my insecurity comes another, equally harsh one: He was very sophisticated about manipulating that aspect of me.

I open my eyes. I'm still here in the marina, which comes as a bit of a surprise. I feel cold despite the sun. I wrap my arms around myself, as if reassuring a scared child. I am a scared child.

Will stands a ways down the dock, waving at me. I force my feet to move.

When I'm finally abreast of him, I see what he's standing by.

It's a motorboat. Shiny and white with sleek lines and a smart-looking cabin.

Annie O' My Heart is emblazoned on the prow in royal blue paint.

CHAPTER TWENTY-NINE

WILL

That instinct to protect Annie kicks in again. She's been a mess today, barely holding it together (not that I blame her). But when she sees Justin's pet name for her on the motorboat, her steps falter and she goes pale. I ease her down into a sitting position in a patch of shade, and she waves me away, burying her head between her knees.

I examine the boat. It's beautiful, white and sleek. Sun glints off the water, casting a dappled shadow against the side of the boat. The cabin door is secured by a padlock with a numbered keypad.

"Wait here," I order Annie. She doesn't lift her head, but flutters one hand in acquiescence. I stride back to my car and open the trunk. Pull a bolt cutter from my toolbox.

With one mighty *snap* the lock is open, hanging limp and useless. I lift it off the door and push my way inside. I try to fight the ominous feeling that consumes me, but it's as dark as night in the cramped cabin.

I realize I've left my sunglasses on, and whip them away from my face with a nervous laugh at my own expense. My eyes blink to adjust to the dim light. I pull on the shade covering one of the windows and it snaps open, flooding the space with light.

As I take in the pristine, neatly organized space, I realize I'm holding my breath and exhale.

What did I think I was going to find in here?

Racing over to the marina to inspect the boat had seemed like the right idea. But now that I'm here, what am I looking for?

First things first. My throat is parched and I'm sure Annie could use some water. I pull open the mini-fridge with an aggressive, proprietary tug. It's a company boat, after all.

A small fleet of bottled waters and a six-pack of premium beer are nestled inside. Nothing's chilled, but the vacuum seal has kept the contents cool enough. I grab water for Annie and a beer for myself. Looking for a bottle opener, I open a few drawers to find biodegradable TP, a bottle of tequila, and a stack of magazines before hitting pay dirt.

I crack open my beer and take a long swallow. Head outside to hand the water to Annie.

"Thanks," she says. Her color is closer to normal, but something's shifted in her eyes; their light's been dimmed. I fervently wish Justin was alive just so I could kick him in the balls.

Annie drains most of the water in one long pull, her head tilted back, the muscles of her throat working as she swallows. She comes up for air. Sighs. Splashes the remaining water on her wrists.

"Anything else of interest in there?" Annie asks.

"Not so far," I answer. "I decided on libations before investigations."

"You could put that on a T-shirt."

I smile, relieved to see her spirit rising, and offer her a hand. She takes it and I pull her to standing. This time we go into the cabin together.

It's tidy and spare. Everything in its place. The tequila is Justin's favorite brand, but other than that the place is characterless and sterile. Even the magazines are a bland assortment: *Men's Health,* a high gloss motorboat and yachting magazine, *Golf Digest*. None of them are magazines that I knew Justin to read.

The curled mailing label on one of the covers catches my eye:

Thomas Justin Childress
47 Windjammer, Unit C
Marina del Rey, CA 90292

I quickly page through the other magazines. They all bear the same name and address. My stomach drops.

Thomas. Justin's brother's name. Using his dead brother's name as an alias is perverse. If he even *had* a brother.

"Annie," I say, handing her one of the magazines. "What do you think? The name's too close to be a coincidence, right?"

She is silent for a moment. "Look at that address. It seems like the boat might just be the beginning of the surprises Justin left for us," Annie says slowly.

Thomas Justin Childress. There's something about the name that bothers me besides the obvious use of Justin's brother's first name as his own.

And then the answer comes to me. *T. J. Childress*. Of course I know that name. Justin had complained bitterly to me about his old friend T.J., saying they'd been paired up in B school at

Columbia in an entrepreneurship class and together developed what proved to be a prize-winning proposal. The relationship imploded when T.J. betrayed Justin, claiming their idea as his own and creating "trouble" for Justin at the university.

He'd never wanted to say more than that, or explain exactly what the trouble had been. The story had slipped out just a few times right after Justin showed up back in Los Angeles, usually when he'd been drinking and had turned a little maudlin. His betrayal at the hand of someone he'd deeply trusted was part of why he'd come to find me, he'd explained; he *knew* I'd never betrayed him and I never would.

Then his mood would suddenly flip and he'd clap an arm around my shoulders, order another round, smile at a pretty girl. I'd feel pleased and gratified, honored to have won his trust, determined to never let him down. I never thought about *T. J. Childress* again afterward.

I'd better start thinking about him now.

The address on the mailing labels is only a few minutes from the marina. Annie and I don't need to talk about it. We walk in silence back to my car and get in. I start to drive.

For my part, I'm afraid to speak, to unleash the questions raised by "Thomas Justin Childress." If there was never really a T.J. in business school, why would Justin make him up? What did he think he could get out of a fake story about a fake betrayal?

My *loyalty,* I realize with a start. Of course. Justin knew all about my mother's revelation to me about my younger brother. He knew how tormented I was by betrayal. Could he have made up the whole thing to create a bond between us?

Maybe. In any event, it had worked.

I feel a little sick and suspect I look as green as Annie did earlier. I take a couple of big deep breaths as we turn the corner onto Windjammer.

Number 47 is easy enough to find. It's nothing fancy. Six aging units in need of paint on a block where most of the other apartment buildings have been given a makeover.

The on-site manager is also easy to find, a plump, tough woman named Fernanda who looks like she charges for smiles. Fernanda has absolutely no interest in letting two complete strangers into a tenant's apartment. Her heavy eyebrows draw together as she shoos us away with an impatient snort for wasting her time.

"Now what?" Annie asks, chewing on the side of her thumb as we walk back to my car.

"Go back. Try to engage her in conversation."

Annie looks at me skeptically. "You *met* her, right?"

"Women can always find something to talk about. If it was a guy, I'd distract him and you'd do it."

"Do what?"

"Break in." A thrill courses through me as I say the words. I'm committed to a stony path now, one laid by a liar. I'm ready to break the law in order to follow it.

"Will, no. Maybe we should just call the police?" Annie wraps her arms around her body.

"And say what? We discovered Justin had an apartment? That's hardly a matter for the police."

"What about calling a locksmith?"

"Any locksmith will have the same problem Lady Charmalade over there has. Neither one of us has any connection to T. J. Childress."

Annie still looks unsure.

"Look, talk about what shitheads men are, that's always a popular topic with the ladies. I'll have a quick look around and be out in a red-hot minute."

Despite her obvious distress, a half smile quirks her lips. "The *ladies*?"

"I'm pretty sure I can get on top of the garbage bins on the side of the building and get in through a window. Come on, we've come this far."

"We've come this far," Annie gamely parrots, though her expression is still pinched with worry.

"Don't worry, I'll be quick."

She heads back to Fernanda and I stay where I am until I hear the rise and fall of women's voices, a surprisingly delicate giggle from Fernanda. I glide through the alley and around to the side of the building where I'd spotted the trash cans.

Up I go, on top of a blue recycling bin. The lock on the window is a joke. This is almost too easy. I haul up the sash and it screeches noisily. I freeze, heart thudding, and hold my breath, prepared to leap down if I hear a shout.

Annie's laugh floats over to me, a little louder and shriller than normal, but only in a way that someone who knew her would recognize. The flow of conversation continues. *Good girl.*

I hop inside Unit C.

The studio apartment is sparsely furnished, to put it mildly. A folding chair and a camping cot flank a blocky wood coffee table. A Styrofoam cooler sits on top. I flick it open. Beer bottles sit in several inches of water.

A galley kitchen runs the length of one wall. I notice the refrigerator shelving and drawers stacked and leaning against the oven.

I somehow know what I'll see when I open up the refrigerator door even before my hand connects with the handle. But even so I'm not prepared.

When the door swings open, Hayley Hayter's dead blue face stares at me, one eye wide open, the other smashed to bits.

CHAPTER THIRTY

CAROL

I've always liked weddings. They're so infused with possibility and hope, promise and happy prospects.

Before the realities of life set in to warp and shatter our expectations.

My wedding to Mike was a small affair. I had no father or mother to walk me down the aisle, so we opted for a city hall ceremony followed by a luncheon in the private dining room of a nearby steakhouse. Mike's parents covered most of the costs, which made me shy about voicing my opinions. I felt so grateful for Mike, for his sister, who I asked to stand as my maid of honor, and for his parents, who welcomed me so warmly that I accepted their every decision.

I bought my dress off the sale rack at Saks. It wasn't a wedding gown, just a simple cocktail-length white sheath dress with filmy sleeves and a little capelet. My aunt and uncle came to the ceremony with their three little boys, but didn't stay for the lunch, which was probably just as well. We had fourteen at the meal in all, me and Mike, his nuclear family, his mom's best friend and her husband, and a handful of our friends.

We drank champagne toasts and ate rare steaks with baked potatoes and creamed spinach. Our wedding cake was a cannoli tower from a beloved Italian bakery in Greenwich Village. The day was simple and perfect and everything I could have asked for. We took a taxi back to our new apartment just as the first dark fingers of dusk descended. Mike put his arm around me and I rested my head on his shoulder. I'd never felt so safe and happy in my entire life.

Justin's wedding to Annie was, of course, an entirely different kind of event. There was a signature cocktail, made with champagne, elderberry liqueur, and fresh raspberries. Passed appetizers included miniature beef Wellingtons, crab cakes, and fried shrimp sliders. The dinner menu featured a wild greens salad with goat cheese crisps, pasta with morel mushrooms and fresh oregano, yuzu poached sea bass, pressed crispy chicken, *and* beef tenderloin, with sides of wild rice, grilled asparagus, and sliced potatoes layered in casserole with cheese and pancetta.

There was dancing and live music and those funny little performers Justin hired to circulate among the many guests. I couldn't believe that Justin and Annie even *knew* that many people, much less felt sufficiently close to all of them to invite them to a wedding.

It was all a bit over the top for my taste, but Justin was paying for the thing, so I let him do what he wanted. Besides, it gave me a certain amount of prideful pleasure, I admit. My boy was a success in the world; if he wanted to splash out on a lavish wedding, who was I to interfere?

I co-hosted an out-of-towners' dinner the night before the big day with Annie's mother and stepfather, and insisted on paying for the wedding flowers after I learned Annie's folks were paying for the hand-lettered invitations and their mailing costs. Other than that, it was Justin's show.

It struck me then, and does again now, just how similar Annie and I were in that regard. Passive about our own weddings, happy to be led, a direct contrast to the popular notion of the controlling bridezilla who obsesses over every detail. Maybe I can talk to Annie about this; maybe it'll be a way in.

Their wedding was magical, of course. The food delicious, the service excellent, the band amazingly tight. I fucked the drummer during his break, in a shadowy corner of the hotel's garden, hoisting my dress and ripping my pantyhose to give him access. He was sweaty and muscled and banged me like I was one of his drums. It was naughty and exhilarating and over in a matter of minutes.

I left my shredded hose in a flowerbed and rejoined the festivities as the band kicked into a rendition of "Tell Me Something Good," by Rufus and Chaka Khan.

There was a surprise performance by a pair of belly dancers. The wedding cake was a many-tiered construction from L.A.'s most decadent bakery, a different flavor for every layer, luxuriously coated in figured white fondant and festooned with fresh flowers. There was a gift bag for each guest containing an assortment of "Annie & Justin" branded swag: shot glasses, luggage tags, aromatherapy candles, T-shirts.

My eyes search out three of the branded candles that I've arranged around a photograph from the kids' wedding day. Justin and Annie, with me in the middle, posed against a wall of flowering vines. Justin looks sharp and charming in his black suit, snow-white shirt, and pearl-gray tie. Annie's smile looks a little forced, but that could be me reading into things. Her custom dress *is* a little ridiculous; maybe that's why.

I examine my own image. I wore metallic gray silk; the sheen of the fabric caught the light alluringly. I'd had my hair and makeup done professionally, a gift from Justin who'd set me up with a "glam squad" for the weekend. I look pretty, younger than my years, even applying a critical eye. I've always been careful to maintain myself well.

A sigh escapes me as I remember the toast Justin made. He greeted the crowd, warmly addressed Annie, and thanked Will for all of his best-man duties. Then he delivered a love letter to me in which he gracefully addressed Mike's tragic death, our close bond, my many sacrifices on his behalf. He displayed gratitude, grace, compassion, and a loving heart. He ended with a lifted glass and a salute to Mike himself, saying he knew his dad would be proud of how I'd raised his son. My heart just about burst with pride.

Thinking about it now makes my eyes fill with tears.

When the intercom buzzer rings, I startle. I'm not expecting anyone; I have no one left to expect. I press the button to speak to the concierge in the lobby.

"You have visitors, Mrs. Childs," announces Sheryl from the front desk.

"Yes?" I inquire. "Who is it?"

Sheryl's voice drops to a low whisper. "It's a couple of police detectives," she replies. "Should I send them up?"

My head fills with a bright white light.

"Mrs. Childs? Are you still there?" Sheryl's voice crackles through the intercom.

"Sure. Of course. Send them up," I say, before releasing the button.

I take a quick glance around, and do a little straightening: organizing a pile of newspapers, carrying a mug from the coffee table in the living room into the kitchen.

When the doorbell rings, I take a look at myself in the hall mirror before answering. My hair falls in soft waves, my lightweight turtleneck hides the worst of my crepey neck. I look wan and tired, like a woman who recently buried her son. I apply a slick of russet lipstick in an attempt to give my face some color.

I wonder if they have new information on what happened to Justin and my heart quickens, uncertainty and ambiguity being much more difficult mindsets to dwell in than hard facts, no matter how painful those facts may be.

I unlock my front door to discover the detectives are both women, which surprises me. I chide myself for my unconscious bias, but I'm also pleased; I expect women will be more sympathetic to me, and I'm deeply aware of my own fragility in this moment.

They introduce themselves as Detectives Ruiz and Waldstein. I haven't spoken to either one of them before in connection with Justin's death. I ask them in and offer seats, which are accepted, and beverages, which are declined. I perch on the edge of an armchair across from the sofa where the two detectives have settled themselves, and wait for them to lead the conversation.

"Thank you for seeing us, Mrs. Childs," Detective Ruiz launches in. "We know you've recently lost your son and that this must be a difficult time."

"It is," I reply simply.

Ruiz continues. "We just have a few questions."

"Okay."

"What do you know about your son's real estate holdings?"

I can't mask my surprise. Whatever I thought she was going to ask, it wasn't this. "Nothing, really. I mean I didn't know he had *holdings*. He and his wife own a house in Mar Vista. His company rents their space, I believe."

Ruiz makes a note on her little pad. "So, you knew nothing about an apartment? In Marina del Rey?"

I shake my head. "No. But he was very clever about money, Justin. He might have bought a place as an investment, even if he didn't necessarily talk to me about it. What does Annie say?"

Ruiz evades my question by asking another one. "How about a boat?"

"A boat?" My eyebrows shoot up in astonishment. A growing sense of alarm frays my composure. "No. Absolutely not. What's going on? What's this about?" I demand.

Ruiz exchanges a glance with her partner before replying. "I regret to inform you of this, Mrs. Childs. But the body of a young woman was found in an apartment rented by your son, a place he rented using an alias, apparently."

My head spins. *The body of a young woman. An alias.*

"What? Who is she?" I stutter. "Has she been identified?"

"Yes, but we haven't informed the family yet, so I'm afraid I can't release that information just now."

That white light fills my brain again, along with a buzzing sound that competes with Ruiz's voice as she continues her questions:

"Are there any other possible holdings Justin maintained that we don't know about?"

"If I didn't know about the one 'possible holding,' how could you really think I would know about any others?" I snap at her.

The two detectives exchange a glance at the sharpness of my tone. I force a little laugh and a vague apology. "Sorry, this is all a bit much."

Ruiz presses on. "Where did Justin maintain bank accounts?"

"I don't know. You should check with his wife, Annie, regarding his personal accounts. And with his partner, Will Barber, on the business front."

"Was Justin and Annie's marriage solid?"

This question takes me aback and I answer carefully. "Who knows what really goes on between a husband and wife? But yes, I believe their relationship was a good one."

Ruiz picks up the wedding photo of me, Justin, and Annie that I was examining earlier. "Nice-looking couple," she compliments. "It's a damn shame."

I'm not quite sure which "it's" she's referring to, but I'm suddenly desperate to have these two detectives out of my apartment. Unfortunately, they don't seem inclined to leave.

Detective Waldstein takes over, "just to confirm a few facts." She asks questions about Justin's company, his history with Annie, my relocation to Los Angeles. She's more conversational than Ruiz, and I find myself feeling relieved as I answer these relatively simple questions.

I'm proudly outlining the achievements of Justin's company and its soon-to-be launch, when Ruiz's cellphone buzzes. "Excuse me," she says, rising to take the call. I watch as she steps through the doorway into the kitchen, closing the door behind her without asking permission. My hackles rise. It feels like a violation.

"You know, I'm feeling quite tired. Would you and your partner mind if we picked this up another day?" My tone is plaintive, but it's not an act.

Waldstein nods. "Sure," she agrees, snapping her notebook closed. "As soon as Diana's off the phone, we'll be out of your hair."

We sit quietly until Ruiz re-enters the room. "Well," she announces. "We've informed the family, so I can be a little more forthcoming with you, Mrs. Childs."

"Yes? What is it?" My voice sounds tinny and far away to my ears. I'm surprised that Ruiz can even hear me, but she responds so she must.

"The body in your son's apartment is Hayley Hayter. A woman who worked with your son's wife. We have reason to believe she was murdered," Ruiz adds matter-of-factly, fixing me with a reptilian eye.

Oh, Justin. My poor, sweet boy.

CHAPTER THIRTY-ONE

ANNIE

"Mommy!"

The word bursts from my lips as soon as Mom and Santiago arrive on my doorstep, direct from LAX, luggage in tow. I don't think I've called my mother "Mommy" in fifteen years.

The single word cracks open the dam and suddenly I'm sobbing, wrenching, desperate sobs. Mom leads me to the sofa and holds me as Santiago silently carries in their luggage, and then fetches a box of tissues for me and glasses of water for the two of us. He then discreetly retires to the kitchen, leaving Mom and me alone in the living room.

Mom does everything right. Strokes my back and murmurs soothing reassurances as my shoulders heave. Hands me tissue after tissue. Waits patiently.

When my living room floor is littered with a snowdrift of used Kleenex and I'm all cried out, I pull away from Mom's embrace and curl on the sofa, my arms protectively wrapped around my knees. Cinnamon Toast jumps up and wiggles his way onto my belly.

Santiago peeks his head around a corner. He's a man of action, my stepfather. Not so good with open displays of emotion, much less hysterical tears, but he's always there when you
need him.

It occurs to me then. They don't even know the worst of it.
Where do I begin?

"Mom," I whisper. "Hayley Hayter's been murdered. I think
Justin killed her."

Mom's hand flies to her throat. "What are you talking
about?"

I tell them about the boat and the magazines and the apartment and the refrigerator. About the obscene message Hayley's
brother left on my voicemail after the police informed him that
her body had been found.

"Dear god," Mom says.

Santiago mutters expressively in Spanish. I'm not fluent, but
I know enough to know he's cursing. "I always had a feeling . . ." Santiago starts in.

"Did you?" I interrupt. "Because that's the thing that's
making me crazy. How did I not see him for who he was?
How could I have been so epically, phenomenally, incredibly
stupid?"

"You weren't stupid!" Mom cries, always my ardent defender. "He seemed perfect. We *all* loved him! And he loved
you!"

"*Did* he, though?" Bitter bile rises in my throat.

"That's not even all of it." I tell them what Will's learned
about Warren Sax.

After the last word stumbles across my lips, we sit in a long
heavy silence.

Santi is the first one to speak. "I'm going to call Lizzie," he announces.

Mom and I swivel our heads toward him, equally surprised.

"I hate to say it," Santi continues, "but I think Annie's going to need a lawyer, a good one, and Lizzie will know the best."

CHAPTER THIRTY-TWO

WILL

I hang up the phone and raise my eyes to meet Sunil's. I know I should tell him about Warren Sax. But I can't, not quite yet.

After I found Hayley, I called the police. Pacing back and forth, I prayed that they would get there quickly. I was horrified and my mind was racing. What else didn't I know? What other grisly surprises had Justin left in his wake?

I was also torn, knowing I needed to tell Annie about my discovery but wanting to prolong her blissful ignorance for even a few minutes longer.

I texted her to stay put, but she followed my lead and clambered in the window over the recycling bin just as sirens signaled the approach of the cops. I kept her away from the refrigerator and the body, but I'm sure her imagination filled in the blanks.

The police arrived. It was awkward and surreal as we explained the trail that had led us to the apartment. Annie broke down and started crying as she produced a picture of Justin. Fernanda identified him as the lawful tenant. Annie tearfully maintained she could prove she was Justin's widow and heir.

One of the cops recognized Justin from a story about his accident.

In the end, they released us with warnings. *Don't go mucking around where you shouldn't. And don't leave town without informing us.*

I brought Annie back to her place. She was quiet, distant. I tried to talk to her, but she shut me down and said she just needed to sleep, that she had never felt so tired in her life. I stopped pushing. After all, I felt much the same. I was a little worried about leaving her alone, but she insisted.

Despite my exhaustion, I came back to the office.

In the last few hours, Sunil and I have learned many facts, each more disturbing than the last.

For starters, we learned that Justin never got an MBA from Columbia; the school had no record that he ever even *attended*. Nor did anyone named "T. J. Childress" during the years that Justin claimed he'd been enrolled. Moreover, Justin's undergraduate work wasn't done at Yale, as he'd told us, but at a small liberal arts college of minor distinction in a far pocket of Connecticut.

But his "inflated" credentials are the least of it.

In addition to the boat purchased on the company's dime, we've unearthed a trove of credit card accounts, taken out under my name and authority, all with screamingly large balances, none of which I knew about.

"A dick move, for sure, that Justin took them out under your name," Sunil says, seeking to reassure me, "but they're company cards, so you have no personal liability. And we're weeks away from launch. It could just be a cash flow problem, particularly since we're due for our next infusion from Sax any day now."

I ask Sunil to confirm some details about how Sax funded us, doing my best to keep the inquiry sounding offhand. He substantiates my understanding: We supplied ninety-day cash flow estimates and the money was direct deposited into Convincer's corporate account.

"At least there hasn't been any problem with that." Sunil sighs. "The money always shows up. Do you think it'll be different now, you know, because Justin was so hands-on with Sax . . ." The corners of his brown eyes crease with worry.

I have to stifle the hysteria that threatens to spill out of me. To say Justin was "hands-on" with Sax is a gross understatement. While he'd freely relayed the story of how he'd impressed Sax and then quit to go out on his own, he'd fiercely guarded the contact, dealing with him directly, claiming it was because of Sax's legendary proclivity for flying under the radar with his investments. Now I know it was all bullshit.

But if Warren Sax, reclusive tech billionaire, isn't funneling money into our company every ninety days, who the hell is?

I realize Sunil is staring at me. I clear my throat, trying to conjure words, but am saved by a knock on my closed office door. I rise and open it.

Molly. Perhaps the last person I want to see right now.

"Hey," I manage. "How're you doing? This isn't really a great time." I gesture to Sunil, who gives Molly a smile that looks like a grimace.

"I think you want to talk to me," she says with an edge. It's not like her and I'm taken aback.

"Okaaaay," I answer. "Sunil? Can you give us a minute?"

Sunil gathers up his laptop and a sheaf of papers, exiting my office without a word. I usher Molly into the pink room with its baby yellow carpet, conscious for the first time in a long time of the absurdity of the color scheme.

"Like I said, babe, it's not really a good time," I start in, but Molly cuts me off.

"How could you?" She stares at me balefully.

"How could I *what*?" I don't have the time or energy for a fight right now, and Molly seems determined to pick one.

"I know about you and Annie."

"What the hell are you talking about?"

"Justin wrote me an email," she says triumphantly. "I got it this morning. He told me you two were sleeping together and his heart was broken."

Reeling over the accusation, I fix on the detail of an email from a dead man. "What do you mean you got it this morning?"

Molly looks at me with something like pity. "He wrote it and scheduled it to send later, which turned out to be after he died."

"It's not true," I answer, but I'm so thunderstruck by Molly's words that even to my ears the words sound feeble.

"Right," Molly says with contempt. "Keep lying. I always knew about you and Annie, on some level, and I don't know why you feel the need to keep up the pretense now that the obstacle to your grand love affair is out of the way. I hope you two will be very happy. You can dance on Justin's grave together."

Now that she's said her piece, her angry bristle is gone. She looks sad and defeated as she gathers herself up to leave my office.

I don't want to fight for Molly; her acceptance of Justin's accusation is the last straw on a camel's back that was already buckling. But I also don't want her to leave just yet either. We were never going to be right together long term, but we had some good times. I put a gentle hand on her shoulder.

She wheels around, her face flushed with anger. "Don't touch me! I wasted almost a year of my life on you!"

"It isn't true," I say softly. "You and I had our problems, but they were ours. They didn't have anything to do with Annie."

"When are you going to give up the charade, Will? Justin told me *everything*! How he bailed *you* out in business school, not the other way around, but how he let you rewrite history because he felt sorry for you! How you begged him to come aboard this company after you were fired from your last gig. How he discovered that not only were you fucking his wife, but that you had embezzled so much money from the company that the whole thing was going to implode!" She gestures expressively. "And now Justin's dead, which is very convenient for you, isn't it?"

I stare at her helplessly. He's framing me.

My throat constricts. There are a million things I want to say, but I find I can't speak.

"You as good as killed him," Molly rages on. "Maybe you did. I'm taking Justin's email to the cops."

I find my voice. "None of that is true. None of it."

"They say every good liar starts with lying to himself," she snaps back. "Good luck."

And she's gone.

My legs are trembling, an involuntary judder. I sink back into my desk chair and push the meat of my palms onto my thighs in an attempt to make it stop.

Whatever Justin was up to, he planned to leave me holding

the bag. The unalterable truth that I was thoroughly and completely played is so profound and enormous that I can barely breathe.

Molly's final words ring in my ears: *"They say every good liar starts with lying to himself."* My challenge is that I don't have a clue where Justin's lies begin or end.

CHAPTER THIRTY-THREE

CAROL

In response to my push on the bell, Santiago answers Annie's door.

I'm surprised to see him; I didn't think he and Laura were back yet. I'm glad for Annie's sake, but disappointed for my own; I'd hoped to see my daughter-in-law alone.

"Carol" is Santiago's minimalist greeting. He stands blocking the doorway.

"Hi," I reply, smoothing my black linen tunic with my palms. "Welcome back. I was hoping to see Annie?"

"She's napping," Santiago answers. He steps outside to talk to me, leaving the front door only slightly ajar.

I've never had a problem with my in-laws. Laura and Santiago are nice enough; he does something I don't understand in IT; she works as an ESL instructor. We've shared many dinners and outings organized around and by the kids. But something has clearly shifted; he hasn't offered even a single word of condolence about Justin's death or apologized for missing the funeral.

Tears well in my eyes. They're genuine, god knows, but I

also hope they'll have an impact. I steal a look at Santiago to see if he's moved by my sorrow, but he remains cold as ice. My back stiffens, and I pull myself up to my full height. Even so, he towers over me, an implacable barrier.

"Annie and I have a bond, you know," I assert. "We both just lost someone we loved dearly. I don't know if you're just jet-lagged or what, but there is absolutely no reason to be rude."

Santiago slides on a pair of mirrored sunglasses. I see my image reflected back at me as he replies, "Just how much do you know about the lies your son fed to our daughter? I find it hard to believe you were completely in the dark."

"I don't know what you're talking about! Can I at least come in and have a glass of water? Talk things over?" I entreat. "It's hot as hades out here."

One of Santiago's bushy eyebrows shoots up over the rim of his aviator frames. He takes his time, but finally gestures me inside. "Be my guest," he says in a tone that's anything but welcoming. "But Annie and Laura are both out cold and I'm not waking them up."

The shadowy darkness of the hallway is a relief after the heat outside. I head for the kitchen, and fill myself a glass of water from the dispenser in the corner. I swallow it down and fill another as Santiago watches me warily, aviators now slung in the collar of his golf shirt.

"Like I said, Annie and Laura are sleeping," Santiago says. "But you didn't answer my question."

"It was vague, to be honest. Can you be more specific? Because I'm not really sure I know what you're talking about."

"Okay. Let's start with this: Did Justin have a brother named Thomas?"

"Oh, that. No."

"What do you mean, 'oh, that'? You knew he lied about having a brother?"

"It's all so long ago, it hardly seems to matter. Back when Justin was just starting business school, he went through a rough patch. He ended up taking some time off to take care of himself and corrected course, but he was embarrassed about falling behind, so he made up a little story."

"Uh-huh. A little story." Santiago is staring at me. He's not asked me to sit. I do so anyway, defiantly curling into a kitchen chair and sipping at my water.

"Aren't we all entitled to go through a hard time and come out the other side?" I press. "Is your life a completely open book?"

"What does a 'rough patch' mean?" Santiago fixes me with dark, glinting eyes. "What happened exactly?" He folds his arms across his chest and leans against the doorjamb.

"I don't see why you're digging up that old history now . . ."

"I don't see why you're *not*." His voice is icy. "Whatever happened, Justin invented a drug-addicted sibling, and then *pretended he died* to cover it up."

"Okay, then. I don't know why you're so fixated on something that happened years ago, but he had a bit of a breakdown. He was institutionalized for a while, actually. Did ECT."

Santiago's eyebrow shoots up again, and I continue, "Shock treatments. Surely you can see why he would want to keep that period of his life private? People don't always understand about mental illness; there's a stigma."

"But why make up a story about a brother who doesn't exist?"

"The shrinks said he was transferring his pain to someone else." I shrug. "Look, I just want to talk to Annie. The police came to see me. They told me about poor Hayley. I know Annie must be really hurting right now."

"I'd say that's an understatement. You do realize Justin is the number one suspect in Hayley's death, right, Carol? And that he was probably having an affair with her?" His face contorts in a snarl. "Annie, our Annie, was living with an unfaithful killer! Driving off that cliff is the most decent thing Justin did in his entire life!"

"I'm not going to let you talk about my son that way!" I retort as I rise and slam my water glass down on the kitchen table. "He didn't kill Hayley!"

"You're deluded."

"And you're being cruel. Justin was a human being, just like the rest of us. He had his weaknesses and faults, he wasn't perfect, he made mistakes. And yes, maybe occasionally he twisted the facts a little to make himself look better, but who hasn't? He was a *good* man and a good husband. Not a killer!"

"I think you should go now" is Santiago's chilly reply.

"I think you're right," I shoot back in a tone as frigid as his. "But you can relay a message to Annie for me. Tell her *I know* Justin was faithful to her. And that no matter what she hears, or surmises, the truth is that he loved her."

Santiago snorts in response. "You think she gives a shit anymore? She's just praying that whatever crap your son was involved in doesn't swallow her alive."

I struggle to keep my composure but I don't want to say things I'll regret later. My eye catches Justin's favorite blue mug in the dishrack and my heart wrenches all over again.

"Just tell Annie I came by," I choke out as I stride past him and toward the front door. Then I stop and address him once more. "You know we should be united now, a *family,* not picking apart the past and leveling unfounded, hurtful accusations at each other."

"I feel sorry for you." Santiago's voice is so soft I can barely hear him.

"I don't need your pity," I retort. "You'll see. Justin will be cleared. You'll be apologizing to me."

"Nothing would make me happier," Santiago replies as he shuts the front door behind me with a decisive *click.*

I slip on my sunglasses and head for my car. The jacarandas are blooming and the street's canopied in rich purple, the pavement dappled with sunshine and welcome shade. It's an idyllic little block, small neat houses, nicely maintained yards. A man and his son come toward me, the father walking, the little boy riding a tricycle. The father's absorbed in his phone; he's paying absolutely no attention to the fact that his son has bicycled far out in front of him.

The boy is abreast of my car. His father half a block away, still enrapt in his electronics. I could open my car door, scoop that child up, and spirit him away without his father even noticing.

People are so pathetic. They don't realize how temporary everything is, how quickly their sense of order in the universe can be upended, their life destroyed.

I should snatch that little boy, just to teach his father a lesson. Sweep him up, tuck him into my car, and drive away.

The boy is mere feet in front of me now, pedaling furiously, his face scrunched with effort.

Just then his dad looks up from his phone. "Andy!" he shouts. "Slow down there, buddy!"

I press my key fob to power open my door locks. Give Andy's unruly hair a swift caress as I pass him, but climb into my car, leaving the child be.

I never would have taken him. Not really. I know what it is to lose a child. I couldn't do it to someone else, even to teach them a lesson.

But I can't be punished for fantasies.

CHAPTER THIRTY-FOUR

ANNIE

When I wake, I feel sluggish and dazed; my tongue is thick in my mouth. Mom's still fast asleep, curled behind me, one arm thrown protectively over my middle. I pull my cell over from the night table. After tapping at my phone with confusion for a few minutes, I realize I've slept for almost twenty-four hours.

I extricate myself from Mom's embrace without waking her and head downstairs. Cinnamon Toast weaves around my ankles, mewing plaintively. I give his head a rub and pour some food into his bowl.

Justin's tiny home office, a screened-in porch with no insulation, is right off the kitchen. That had been another planned project of ours, finishing the room, making it truly all weather.

It's searingly hot outside again today; the room is stuffy and too warm even with the blinds pulled shut. I sink into Justin's desk chair and give it a little swivel. I never came in here much; it was always Justin's domain. I sniff the faint scent of him that lingers, spicy, sweet, very male.

There's a picture of me on his desk, a candid shot he snapped one day when we were on a hike. My hair is tousled, my cheeks pink with exertion, my sunglasses perched atop my head. I'm smiling, happy, innocent. I gently lay the frame glass-side down on the desk.

I flip open his laptop. Password protected. I try a few random guesses: his birthday, "password," our anniversary, my name, Carol's. No go.

I turn my attention to his desk drawers. The top one holds no surprises: pens, crumpled singles and a handful of change, assorted business cards, paper clips, a spare phone charger, a stress ball, the card I wrote him on our anniversary. I read the words I'd labored over so carefully.

Darling J,

One whole year! I can hardly believe it. The past 365 days have flown by. As we've taken the first few wobbly steps into building our future together, I've come to love you more with every passing day. You make me want to be better; you actually make me better just loving you. You restored an elemental faith in myself that I thought I'd lost forever and for that I will always be grateful. May every anniversary we share be as blissful as this one.

Love, A

The card's face depicts a stick figure groom carrying a stick figure bride over the threshold of a stick figure home. The reference to the *wobbly steps* was a private joke, a reference to the uneven front stairs at our little cottage, a joke that now leaves a bitter taste. It was just over six months ago that I wrote those words.

Stupid fool that I am.

fool [ˈfül]

> ***noun,*** a silly or stupid person
>
> **synonyms:** nitwit, simpleton, dunce, ninny, cretin, nincompoop, dolt, idiot, jackass, buffoon, blockhead, numbskull, oaf, boob, clod, dunderhead, ignoramus, imbecile, moron, driveler, bonehead, etc.

The synonyms for *fool* are almost endless, and I deserve to be labeled with every single one.

But no more. My eyes are wide open now.

The next drawer contains stacks of files, each one neatly labeled: *Amex, Visa, Discover, Verizon, AAA, Car Insurance, Life Insurance, Mortgage,* etc. I start at the top and work my way down.

It's ugly. There are multiple credit card accounts I knew nothing about. Many of them are in my name. All of them are past due, with enormous balances largely accrued through cash advances, accumulating interest at a nauseating clip.

There are *three* mortgages on our house, two of them sporting my *forged* signature. There's a copy of the lease for the apartment on Windjammer, signed with Justin's distinctive, illegible autograph, in a file marked *Research*.

I marvel at his sheer *audacity*. Every bit of it was just sitting here, neatly organized and labeled, under our shared roof. If I'd been even the slightest bit nosy, I would have unearthed it all. I shiver despite the heat as I realize that it's technically not even our roof. Three different banks own this house, not me.

I don't understand, and I don't think I ever will. Not only *how* he pulled it off, but *why* he felt compelled to in the first place. We were doing fine with our two salaries; we could have made our nut on mine alone if we were careful.

I used to tease Justin about living large and splashing out, even as I welcomed his generosity. I thought I understood his largesse: He was a self-made man, who appreciated the fragility of good fortune and wanted to share his with others. It seemed genuine.

Could it have *been* genuine, despite his being a liar and a cheat? Possibly a *killer*?

The contours of the room swim before my eyes. More hot tears. I'm impatient with myself; *what am I grieving exactly*? The loss of Justin? Or the enormity of his betrayals?

I hear the front door open. The sound of Santiago's gravelly voice floats in, along with another voice it takes me a moment to place.

Bella. My heart lifts a little.

I exit Justin's office and head for the kitchen. There I find Santiago unloading cartons of savory, mouthwatering take-out while Bella grabs plates and utensils from drawers.

"You're awake!" Santiago announces.

"You don't miss a trick," I reply, trying to match his jovial tone.

Bella wraps her arms around me from behind. "How're you doing, sweetheart?" she murmurs into my uncombed hair.

"I've been better," I reply weakly. Suddenly I'm ravenous. I grab a plate and load it up: garlic chicken, plantains, rice and beans, Cuban food at its most delicious. I stuff my mouth.

Bella arches an eyebrow at me as I wipe a smear of garlic sauce from my chin. "Slow down, girl," she teases. "The food's not trying to escape."

I swallow down a mouthful of sweet plantain. Bella hands me a glass of cold water and I drain it.

"Thank you." I nod at both Santi and Bella. I do feel marginally better, but a heavy silence falls over the three of us. Santiago picks at a chicken wing, shredding it meticulously. Cinnamon Toast leaps up onto the counter and eyes the chicken fragments with rapt attention.

I'm the one to break the silence. "Bella, when Justin and I first got together you were the only one who spoke up—"

"Oh, sweetheart," she interrupts. "We don't need to go into that ancient history! Not now."

"I have my reasons for asking you, Bell. I know I shut you down back then, but now I need you to be honest with me. You were pissed when Justin ghosted me, but was there anything else?"

"It was a long time ago." Bella hesitates, twisting her hair into spirals. "How can it really matter?"

"Please! Just tell me."

"Okay. Okay." She shrugs. "Here it is: that weekend you met Justin up at Mammoth? I'm not sure it was entirely an accident."

"What are you talking about? I totaled my car."

"Right. I know there was *an accident*. But . . . well, the first day we were on the slopes, I met Justin. We started talking, and he was so charming. You know better than anyone how he could be." Bella shrugs again.

"So, you met him. So what?" There's a defensive bristle in my reply and Bella casts her eyes away from mine.

"I pointed you out. I said that you were in need of a fun weekend."

"Wow. I had no idea you thought I was so pathetic!"

Bella jerks back, stung, and Santiago raises his hands, asking for peace. "We know you're really hurting, honey," he says. "But just hear Bella out."

Bella shoots him a grateful glance. "I didn't think you were pathetic. He was with a group of cute guys and I thought we'd *all* hang out. I was just flirting. It was before I wiped out and hurt myself."

"Okay. Again—so what?"

"Okay. Here it is. He didn't seem all that interested in you—like he was just being polite, you know? Until I mentioned that you worked at MediFutur. Then it was like a switch flipped. So much so that it struck me as a little weird at the time. But then, you know, I got hurt and forgot all about him, and then he was your knight in shining armor, with the car. I told myself I'd imagined it."

Bella's arms raise and drop. I can tell she feels better for getting this admission off her chest.

On the other hand, *my* chest feels like it might explode.

My job. He was interested in me because of *my job*.

It was the answer I was searching for but still I'm in the dark.

"Tell me everything."

Bella looks startled. "What do you mean?"

"How did MediFutur come up?"

"I don't know, exactly, it was years ago!"

"Try to remember, Bell. You pointed me out, how did that happen?"

"I was flirting with one of his friends, that guy Darien he used to hang with?"

I nod. Darien was a peripheral friend of Justin's who fell away after we got serious.

"Anyway. He asked who I was there with. Said he was with friends and maybe we could all meet up later."

"Where was this?"

"By the lift. We figured out that we were all from L.A. I think maybe it came up then. You had just gotten that piece placed in the *L.A. Times* so I was bragging on you."

"And that's when Justin became interested?"

"Bingo. And, oh, right! He wanted to know if you were just P.R. or if you understood the science. I told him you were a word nerd from way back." Bella shrugs. "Anyway, like I said, weird at the time, and then . . ." She trails off with another shrug.

My mind races. I am a word nerd.

But Hayley was a tech nerd.

Bella and Santiago are looking at me, I realize, warily gauging my reaction. Bella twirls her hair. "Are you mad at me?"

It surprises them both when I begin to laugh.

CHAPTER THIRTY-FIVE

WILL

I suppose I ought to be grateful that Vern Fellowes, the CEO of MediFutur, is even willing to see me.

It might be curiosity motivating him. Or pity. I'm not sure, but if our positions had been reversed, I probably would have declined. The speculation that the husband of one employee killed another employee in a sordid love triangle is hardly the kind of P.R. a company like MediFutur wants.

Nonetheless, here I am, in their stark, modern waiting area, fifteen minutes early for my appointment.

There's an easel in one corner holding a large photograph of a smiling Hayley and an announcement about an upcoming memorial in her honor. It conjures another image: her cold blue face, her shattered eye. I pluck at a loose thread on the edge of my shirt so as not to look at the poster.

I think about texting Annie to see how she's doing, but when I last called, her mother picked up and said Annie was finally sleeping. I rub my own eyes and stifle a yawn. Each time I've tried to sleep, a sudden adrenaline flare floods my system right before I doze off, jerking me back to an uneasy wakefulness. I'm exhausted. I'm wired.

The loose thread comes away from my shirt in a satisfying spiral.

Then Fellowes's assistant is asking me in, offering me beverages as he escorts me down the hallway to a sunlight-flooded corner office. My eyes blink rapidly to adjust to the light.

To my mild surprise, Fellowes isn't alone. There's a sleekly dressed woman sitting in one of the two deep, square armchairs that flank his desk.

Lawyer is my guess.

A prickle races down my spine. Maybe this meeting isn't so friendly, after all.

My instinct is proven correct. The woman introduces herself as Lorraine Perkins, general counsel for MediFutur. Her voice is pure steel.

I begin by offering condolences about Hayley. Fellowes cocks an eyebrow and exchanges a glance with his attorney. "What is it you want, Mr. Barber?" Fellowes demands. "Unless you're here to return our property I don't think we have anything to discuss."

"Return your property?" I'm completely bewildered, but dread seeps through my veins like a London fog, thick, slow, and pervasive.

"Surely you're not going to start playing the innocent now?" Fellowes looks genuinely affronted.

"I honestly don't know what you're talking about."

"That's it, then," Lorraine clips out. "You should be advised that we've launched a full investigation and intend to turn over all of our findings to the police."

Two burly security guys materialize in the doorway, summoned like genies.

I'm not an idiot. I stand and gesture surrender. It's time to go.

They think I have something that belongs to them.

My brain is spinning, but this explains a lot. If Justin wasn't with Hayley for sex, maybe he was with her for something she stole from MediFutur.

With a lurching stomach I remember when he accelerated our launch a few months ago, based on the "latest breakthrough by Dylan, our resident genius." What if Dylan's breakthrough had, in fact, been appropriated illegally by Justin?

I'm outside now; the guards have deposited me directly in front of MediFutur's concrete cube of a building. Harsh sun forces me to squint. I slide on sunglasses and head for my car.

Twenty minutes later I'm back in Venice, at the Convincer offices. There's a desperate mad-tea-party atmosphere among our employees. Music's blaring. Huddled groups splinter when I enter, nervous-looking people hurtling back to their desks. Rumors must be flying thick and fast, and they don't even know the half of it. The staff tries to straighten up and fly right when they see me, but an edge of hysteria colors everyone.

I head for the lab in search of Dylan, our "resident genius." I've never quite clicked with Dylan; he's got an intensity I find unnerving, probably a result of where he lands on the neurotypical spectrum.

When I ask, I'm informed he's in the meditation room—once a windowless storage for baby clothes, now a yoga-mat-filled retreat for the tech nerds.

I enter without knocking. Dylan's barefoot, cross-legged on

the floor, hunched over a laptop, one hand tugging at his unruly hair.

"Am I interrupting?" I ask.

"Always" is his snarky reply. He doesn't even look up.

"Dylan," I begin, and then stop short. If I'm correct and Justin obtained proprietary tech from Hayley, Dylan must be complicit. Not just in the theft, maybe in her death as well. I can't just come out and accuse him.

I watch as his fingers fly over his keyboard. Once again, he pauses and tugs at his hair. The unpleasant scent of dirty clothes and unwashed man wafts in my direction. I can't tell if he's avoiding eye contact or just being his usual self.

I decide then and there that I've had enough of playing amateur detective. Justin has left me in deep shit, that much is crystal clear. I can't handle this situation on my own.

"Dylan. Look at me," I command.

His eyes flick to me. Dart back to his screen.

"Is there anything you want to tell me, Dylan?"

"Only that if you don't let me get back to work, we'll never hit our launch targets." His fingers are a blur on the keyboard. His eyes glued.

Okay. He's made his choice. I've made mine.

I'm going to the police. I'm going to tell them everything.

CHAPTER THIRTY-SIX

CAROL

I couldn't really make sense of Los Angeles when I first moved here. A sprawling mess of interlocking counties, cities, and villages both official and unofficial, L.A. lacks a sense of order that I took for granted as a New Yorker.

When I was first looking to move to the West Coast, downtown L.A. felt the most like home to me. At least it was a semblance of a city. But the staggering population of homeless living in tent encampments, as well as the distance from the Westside, where Justin and Annie were living, made me rethink.

I settled on the neighborhood of Westwood, and Justin found my apartment. I liked the city feel of the Wilshire Corridor apartment buildings and the proximity to Westwood Village, with movie theaters and shops within walking distance.

It was only after I moved in that I discovered the Village's strange, almost ghostly character. Unable to find shops and restaurants that cater to the student market as well as the affluent residents in the surrounding neighborhood, the Village suffers constant retail turnover. I heard it once had a heyday, but it's long past.

Now it's an odd collection of cheap clothing shops, cookie bakeries, hookah lounges, and chain restaurants, anchored by a pair of large standalone movie theaters that squat opposite each other and are still regularly used for gaudy movie premieres. Many empty storefronts sport FOR LEASE signs.

I discovered that I liked to take long walks through the pedestrian-only sections of the UCLA campus, away from the buses that roared up the main drag of the Village. I could be anonymous, hands tucked into a hoodie, eyes shaded behind sunglasses. On these excursions I found the street theater I so badly missed from New York.

New lovers swooning into each other, students promoting clubs, religious proselytizers, harried-looking professors, peppy tour guides leading eager parents and dazed-looking high school students, an outdoor fencing class, varsity teams out for a jog—I never know what I'll find.

I'm here today, perched on a shaded bench near the statue of the large bear placed on a pedestal between the athletic facilities and the bookstore. Picture-takers snap a series of happy poses with the bear. They flash peace signs or offer thumbs-ups, grin broadly or give shy smiles.

A young man catches my eye. How could he not? He's so like Justin at that age. Those lively eyes, that coiled energy!

A smile lifts the corner of my mouth as I watch him throw an arm around the shoulders of a woman who must be his mother. Shorter than her son by a good six inches, she shares the same thick reddish-brown hair and uptilted nose.

I took this walk with a purpose in mind. I need to clear my head. Think things through and decide on a course of action. I'm wrestling with the horns of a moral dilemma.

I'm in a rare position of power. I've been forced to react to circumstance so much of my life. I know how to cope, adapt, and readapt, but having *options* feels heady and rich.

If I go to the police with the information I have, I will undoubtedly destroy lives. But so what? I'm not responsible for other people's decisions. That's something I learned a long time ago. I can control only my own attitude and my own actions.

I rise and head for the steep stairs at the center of the campus that I know will get my heart rate up. A kid on a skateboard whizzes past me with a wink and a low wolf whistle. His cheekiness flatters and annoys me at the same time.

The stairs loom in front of me, three steep brick flights, so shallow I need to keep my eyes fixed on them as I climb or I stub my big toes every time. The first round leaves me breathless. I tap my way back down and take the three flights up once again.

Sweaty and proud of myself, I pause at the top and rest my hands on my knees. The plaza at the top of the stairs is littered with blue and gold sequins, residue of someone's celebration.

I remember Justin's tenth birthday. Magic themed. His last birthday before Mike died. Robyn was there and Mike's parents, of course. We were still a family then.

We had games and cake and a real live magician, the Magnificent Marvel. He was a huge hit with the kids and with the adults too, possessing an impish charm and patter loaded with slightly naughty double entendres. After all the guests left, Justin disappeared into his room with his presents while Mike and I straightened up the house.

After a good solid hour of picking up paper plates and plastic cups, sweeping crumbs and wrapping leftovers, I finally turned on the dishwasher. Mike pulled the trash out to the curb. We collapsed on the living room sofa. Mike reached for my hand and pulled it to his mouth for a kiss, signaling his appreciation for a job well done. I smiled at him, happy.

Justin appeared, a black mask over his eyes, a black satin cape flung over his shoulders.

"I am Mephisto the Mysterious!" he announced in an attempt at a bass growl. "Behold my magic!"

He ran through a series: Chinese interlocking rings, a card trick, pulling a coin from behind my ear.

Mike and I applauded and Justin rewarded us with a sweeping bow to the ground.

It was past his bedtime and we told Justin to go brush his teeth. Mike and I sat for a few moments more in a companionable silence.

"I'll go check on him," I volunteered.

I found Justin sound asleep on top of his covers, fully dressed, cape still knotted around his neck. I tugged off his sneakers and removed the cape. Pulled his extra blanket over him. His breath was deep and even, his hair falling into his eyes. I smoothed it away and kissed his forehead.

There is nothing like the love a mother has for her child.

Mike was waiting for me in the bedroom, buck naked and smiling. He pulled me into his arms and onto the bed, nuzzling my neck right at the spot he knew drove me *insane*. Our sex was familiar and loving and explosive.

As we crawled under the covers, Mike opened his arms and I nestled my head on his bare chest. He closed his arms around me, almost instantly asleep. I relaxed into the rhythm of his long, deep breaths. I felt safe.

How long has it been since I've felt safe?

"Are you all right, ma'am?" A concerned-looking corn-fed

youth is squinting at me from underneath the brim of a baseball cap.

"What?" I startle. "Oh, I'm fine."

"Okay. It's just that you were, um, breathing really hard. And kind of red in the face."

What business is it of yours? That's what I want to say. Then I soften. At least this is a polite, concerned young man. Better than the many oblivious little shits I've encountered.

"Thank you. Just working out. So that's kind of what I was going for."

"Good for you. At your age!" The dolt smiles at me like this is actually a compliment.

"Have a good one." I smile through clenched teeth as I walk quickly away.

I teeter on the verge of invisibility; I know it. If I didn't work so rigorously to maintain my figure, if I wasn't so careful to dye my hair, I'd be invisible already. But to be an object of leering *and* pitying condescension all in one morning? Horrible.

I circle back to my apartment building. Wave hello to the concierge on duty at the desk. Ride the elevator upstairs.

I'd left the living room window open and a welcome breeze stirs the air. I avoid looking in the hall mirror and head for the kitchen. I gulp a glass of water and take a seat, removing my sneakers. As I rub my feet, I consider my options:

Silence.

An anonymous tip.

Direct communication with the authorities.

Silence hardly seems tenable. The information would fester, sure to rot me from the inside out. And there's the matter of justice. People need to face consequences for their actions or society collapses.

I debate the merits of an anonymous tip. The information would be in the right hands, but how much credence would the police give to information that came from an unnamed source?

I could, of course, contact Detective Ruiz. I'm sure she would appreciate how much easier my information will make her life, enabling her to put a murderer behind bars.

Will Barber charmed me and fooled Justin. He more than likely will make moves on Annie after a "decent" interval too. I think about the bogus credit cards Justin told me about, the forged checks. I'm filled with loathing for Will as I contemplate my options for bringing him to justice.

But is that something I want on my conscience?

There is so much pain in the world, do I really want to rain down more?

CHAPTER THIRTY-SEVEN

ANNIE

Mom nagged until she got me out to work in our tiny back garden. I have to admit she was right to push me. On my knees, with my gloved hands in the dirt and the warm sun on my back, I'm reminded of all that life offers, rather than all it takes away.

She works silently beside me. Turning her spade with a happy little hum. Patting earth around fragile roots and giving each little plant a gentle blast from a misting bottle once it's settled.

Back here in the garden, it's possible to ignore the journalists camped outside my house, the constantly ringing phone, the down-the-rabbit-hole quality that now defines my existence.

I had forgotten what it was like to just feel *at peace*.

The day Justin and I moved in here together was anything but. It was *chaos*. We'd decided it would be romantic to both move in the same day. That meant two crews of movers, one at Justin's old place and one at mine early in the morning, with a plan of arriving at the house together in the early afternoon.

My crew's truck broke down on their way to me. The com-

pany was apologetic but said it would take at least four hours
to dispatch a second team. I called Justin. He was just greeting
his movers, on schedule, his excitement palpable. Frustrated, I
began humping boxes out of my apartment and out to the
front of my building.

I'd moved about half a dozen when it began to rain, fat
drops splattering on the cardboard cartons. I looked at the
sorry collection of boxes. Should I carry them back inside? My
back already hurt and my arms were aching. I began to cry, the
tears rolling down my face as fat as the raindrops.

This move suddenly seemed overwhelming and *wrong*. I felt
irritated that Justin wasn't here to help me. Our romantic,
playful idea to "come together" at our new house now seemed
stupid. We should have moved on separate days and been there
to help each other.

I felt wounded. Abandoned. I nursed that grudge, avoiding
Justin's excited texts and calls about his progress.

abandoned [ə-ˈban-dənd]
   adjective, 1. deserted, forsaken; 2. exuberantly enthusiastic; 3. recklessly unrestrained

By the time my movers showed up and got me to the house,
it was dark. My clothes were soaked through and my hair was
matted to my head. I looked and felt like a drowned rat. I was
deep in the self-indulgent misery of definition number 1, with
an angry pinch of 3.

When I pulled up in front of the house, the moving truck
rumbling behind me, the front door was wide open, creating a
warm, welcoming rectangle of golden light. Justin was framed
in the center, that magnificent merry smile on his face.

He ushered me in and told me to go shower and change while he took charge of the movers. He'd laid out sweats of his for me, he told me; they'd be too big, but they were dry. I gratefully agreed.

A hot shower both calmed and energized me. I climbed into Justin's sweats and felt cozy and comforted by his faint, lingering scent. My irritation and frustration with the day began to fade. I looked around my new bedroom, *our* new bedroom. The new bed we'd purchased together dominated the space. Boxes were still everywhere, of course, but I began to imagine the space put together, the bedroom I'd begin my marriage in.

Barefoot, I padded out into the living room. Justin was directing traffic as movers traipsed in and out of the house.

"Annie O' My Heart," Justin exclaimed. "There you are! I have a housewarming present for you."

He handed me a wrapped box. Heavy. Solid. Inside was a copy of the *Oxford English Dictionary*.

"I remembered." He beamed at me. "The first night we met, when I asked what your favorite book was, and you said no house was a home without one."

I ached with love for him in that moment. Couldn't even fathom the irritation I'd harbored earlier. Couldn't wait for the movers to get out of the house so I could fuck him senseless.

A shadow looms over me and Mom, pulling me back to the here and now. I look up, expecting Santiago.

It's Hugh Hayter.

I scramble to my feet, my heart pounding in my chest.

"What are you doing here? How did you get in?" I stammer.

"I came in the gate, if you must know. It was unlatched," he replies defensively. "I closed it behind me so the journos couldn't follow. You should thank me."

Mom doesn't know who he is, but is on her feet now too, always instantly protective of me.

"This is Hugh Hayter, Hayley's brother," I inform her so she understands my alarm.

"I'm going to have to ask you to leave the property, Mr. Hayter," Mom announces in her most schoolteacher voice. "I heard that message you left my daughter, and it was disgusting."

Hugh colors. "That's why I'm here," he admits. "This has been really hard on all of us, and I realize my anger at you may have been misplaced. You're as much a victim in all this as me and my family. I came to apologize."

"Thank you for that," I reply, relieved. In his infamous phone message, torture and death were deemed too good for me, the person who had introduced Justin into Hayley's life.

Hugh's eyes fill with tears, infusing me with an entirely different sense of alarm. I'm not handling my own grief particularly well; I can't take on his.

Fortunately, Mom catches my eye and takes charge, escorting Hugh into the house for a cup of tea. Knowing Mom, she'll put a shot of whiskey in it for "medicinal purposes."

I linger in the garden on the pretense of putting tools away, but really just taking the time to pull myself together.

My momentary sense of peace fragments into tatters. Hugh's sudden arrival has left me on edge, vulnerable and uneasy. The immediacy of the scandal may fade, but Justin's story—and mine—will no doubt be the subject of tabloid articles for months if not years to come. I imagine the actress hired to play a lightly fictionalized version of me in a Lifetime movie, overemoting as a serious-sounding narrator outlines Justin's many transgressions.

I start to laugh. Maybe it's a gift. Maybe I can leverage my personal tragedy into a book deal. Who better to write this story than me? My writer brain begins spinning.

Perhaps I can explore how Hugh and I are forever bound by tragedy. Two strangers brought together in pain, anger, and grief, who forge an unshakable bond and . . . do what? I don't know the ending to that story, but I'm relieved to find myself asking questions about how to start a new one. Despite everything, I feel a flutter of resilient hope. It's good Hugh came here today. The start of a healing.

I take myself inside. I feel giddy, buoyed by a momentary fantasy of a book tour and glowing reviews touting my "fearless honesty" and "deft command of language."

Hugh's at the kitchen table, in what was Justin's usual seat. It unsettles me briefly, but, of course, there's no way Hugh could have known.

Mom's by the stove, setting tea bags into mugs. After washing my hands, I grab a coffee cake from the counter and set about cutting a few hefty slices.

"How are your parents doing?" I ask, as I arrange the cake slices on a plate. "I mean, I know, *shitty,* but are they okay?"

Hugh caves as if I'd punched him. "My mother's checked into a *facility,*" he says in low, anguished tones. "I won't see her for at least thirty days. So, no. They're not okay."

"Oh god. I'm so sorry." I mean it, but the words sound woefully thin. I avert my eyes and reach for foil to cover the cake, just to give myself something to do.

"Chamomile for you, honey?" Mom asks me, turning away from the stove. She freezes. A tiny gasp escapes her as her hand flies to her throat.

I follow her line of sight. Hugh has a gun in his hand, an

ugly gray thing with a pugnacious snout. He claps it down onto the Formica top of my kitchen table with a *thunk*.

"My family is destroyed," he laments. "Broken. Hayley was . . . the light. The glue."

"People heal from grief," Mom says kindly, wary eyes on Hugh's weapon. "It takes time, though. You have to give it time."

"I can't heal from this. It's too much." Hugh's pained voice is so soft I have to strain to hear him.

"Come on, Hugh," I entreat. "I mean, I understand, you know I do, but I'm not *giving up*." My eyes dart over to meet Mom's. She gestures at me to keep talking.

"Why don't you give me that gun?" I say soothingly. "I'll give it back to you when you leave."

"I'm not stupid," Hugh growls.

"Of course not!" Mom rushes to assure him. "No one said you were."

"It's just a house rules kind of thing," I continue. "No big deal. I'll put it in our gun safe until you're ready to leave."

"You have a gun safe?" Hugh looks at me with interest.

Of course not.

"Of course I do," I answer him firmly. His eyes narrow suspiciously. "For guests. Guests with guns." I hold his gaze steadily, clinging to my fiction despite my hammering heart.

"She was *good*, you know, Hayley. She was the *best* person." Hugh wails.

"I know," I reply softly. "She was my friend. I miss her too."

"Why didn't he kill you?" Hugh demands, grabbing the gun and pointing his weapon directly at my face.

Words choke in my throat. I honestly don't know why the

fuck Justin *didn't* kill me. He might as well have. And it sure looks like Hugh is going to finish the job for him.

"I don't know why he didn't kill me," I manage to whisper. "But let my mother walk out of here, and we can talk about it. Justin was *my* husband. This is *my* problem."

Mom's face is white, but she shakes her head at me vigorously, indicating there's no fucking way she's leaving me alone with this maniac.

I raise my hands in a gesture I hope is placating. "Hugh. I know you're hurting. Believe me, I know. But this won't solve anything. You should walk out of here, go home, and try to sleep. You must be exhausted! Right? I know it's all hit me that way. When you get some rest, you'll see things differently."

"What was it all for?" His voice is strangled by emotion. His extended arm is shaking. My eyes follow the barrel of the gun like it's a bouncing ball.

It takes me a moment to understand what he means. Then it hits me: *Why* are Haley and Justin dead? *Why* is his family destroyed?

"I wish I knew," I reply truthfully.

He nods at me, his eyes wide with what seems like understanding. He drops his arm so the gun is pointing at the floor. I exhale.

Out of the corner of my eye, I see Mom dialing 911 on her cellphone as she creeps toward the hallway. The tinny voice of the dispatch operator crackles to life over the phone's speaker. "Nine-one-one. What's your emergency?"

Hugh rears up at the sound of the dispatcher's voice. Raises his gun again.

"No!" The word explodes from Mom's lips.

Hugh turns the muzzle of the gun away from me and toward his own skull.

"Hugh! Don't do it!" I yell. "Please!"

He pulls the trigger. Brains, blood, and skull fragments splatter against my cheery yellow kitchen wall.

Hope dies.

CHAPTER THIRTY-EIGHT

WILL

Sunil and I have put together as many pieces of the puzzle as we can. I'm astonished really, at how completely devoted to Justin we all were, how we never noticed it was all a scam. A house of cards built on lies, deception, and fraud, now all tumbling to the ground.

I feel a sense of relief, actually. Finally, I know the worst and can face it squarely. And we think we have enough to exonerate me, no matter what Justin emailed to Molly.

"I've got your back all the way." Sunil's dark brows knit together. "You ready, man?"

"No time like the present," I agree, as I stand and reach for my jacket.

There's a knock on my closed door.

"Come in," I call. It's Ginny, our receptionist. She's agitated and bounces back and forth on her platform sneakers.

"Uh, Will, the police are here. *Detectives.*"

Sunil shoots me a surprised glance. "Mountain to Mohammed," he mutters.

"All right," I instruct Ginny. "Tell them to come in."

I remove my jacket and settle back into my chair. Sunil gives me a reassuring nod.

Two women in plain clothes enter, followed by two male cops in uniform. It seems a little excessive.

"Will Barber?" one of the women asks.

"Yes. That's me. I'm glad you're here, Officer."

"Detective," she corrects. "Detective Diana Ruiz. And why's that?"

"I was just coming to make a report. I have evidence that my deceased partner was involved in massive financial fraud."

Ruiz pins me with her sharp, dark eyes. Sweat breaks out on my forehead. "I, we." I gesture to Sunil. "This is Sunil Bhatti, our CFO. The two of us are guilty of stupidity, but nothing more. And we have the paper trail to prove it."

"I'll be interested to hear all about it, Mr. Barber."

There's something in Ruiz's tone that unsettles me.

"What brought you here today?" I ask cautiously.

"Funny you should ask." Ruiz's eyes bore into mine. "Will Barber, you're under arrest for the murders of Justin Childs and Hayley Hayter."

I feel the blood drain from my face.

"What?" Sunil leaps to his feet, incredulous. "That's ridiculous!"

Ruiz goes on to read me my rights. Sunil promises he'll find the best attorney money can buy. I tell Sunil to call Annie, and also not to tell my mother under any circumstances. I assure him this is a massive mistake and that it will all be sorted out.

It feels completely unreal as they handcuff me, actually *handcuff me,* and perp walk me out in front of my already devastated staff.

I take it in, along with the shocked and dismayed faces of

the people in the office. This is all ending. Right here. Right now. I never thought my downfall could be so swift and complete.

A sudden pounding at my right temple nearly blinds me. A migraine? A stroke? I stumble as we exit the building and one of the uniformed cops grips my elbow.

There's a waiting panda patrol car, cherries lazily spinning. I'm escorted into the backseat, my head cradled by a uniform's meaty hand.

CHAPTER THIRTY-NINE

CAROL

The waiting room at St. John's is thronged with the anxious; I'm among them, slouched in a corner, a hat pulled low over my face.

Annie's been admitted to this hospital in the wake of Hugh Hayter's suicide. That's all I've been able to learn thus far. He's dead and she's here.

Like a *stranger,* I was reduced to hearing about this latest tragedy on the news. No one bothered to call me.

The story of Hugh's death has caught flames and the press is fanning them, so I have *some* information, but its accuracy is questionable. I need to see Annie for myself. Make sure she's all right. Make sure she understands. She's all I have left.

Santiago emerges from an elevator with two Starbucks cups and I slouch a little lower. He disappears down the hallway. I deflate, but perk up when he re-emerges with Laura. They take their coffees and disappear in the opposite direction.

It's now or never. I casually make my way down the corridor. Most of the doors are half-open, revealing beds occupied by patients in various states of misery. But I'm in luck. Annie is revealed dozing in a room where the second bed is empty. I enter and close the door softly behind me. I pull off my hat and take a seat in the chair next to the bed.

She looks fine, as far as I can tell. No bandages or bruises, at least none visible. Her mouth is partly open, giving her a vulnerable, childlike appearance. I heave a sigh of relief.

I wish Annie and I could start again. We both loved Justin so much, shouldn't that be a foundation for *something*?

Aware that I probably have limited time, I lay a gentle hand on Annie's shoulder.

"Annie. Hi, honey. It's Carol."

Her eyelids flutter open. "Where's my mom?"

"Just down the hall having a coffee with Santiago."

I can't say I like the anxious look in Annie's eyes.

"I won't stay long," I promise. "I just had to see for myself that you were okay! What a terrible, terrible thing. You're not hurt, right?"

"No. They said I went into shock, but no, I'm fine."

"Thank god! Still. I'm so sorry. That boy must have been in so much pain."

"Yes."

A silence falls. Annie struggles to keep her eyes focused, her head upright.

"They gave me something. To make me sleep," she says, slurring slightly.

"Can I ask what happened? I don't mean to be ghoulish, you know, there's just been so many rumors, and my mind is conjuring just *the worst* . . ."

"He shot himself in the head. In front of Mom and me," Annie interrupts flatly.

"I'm so sorry." My heart aches for her.

"Do you know how long my mom's going to be?" That anxious look is back in Annie's eyes. If only she understood how much I want to be another mother for her. Clearly she needs me just as much as I need her. Maybe in time.

"I hate to be the bearer of more bad news," I say. "But did you hear about Will? The police arrested him for Justin's murder. And that poor girl Hayley's too."

Annie's eyes snap open. I see her fighting through the fog of the medicine. "That's not possible."

"I couldn't believe it either!" I assure her. "I'll be heartbroken if it turns out to be true."

"What evidence do they have? This is crazy! It makes no sense!" Annie sits up abruptly and tries to climb out of the bed, despite the IV drip dangling from her arm.

"Annie. Stop. You're hooked up there, sweetheart," I add, pointing to the IV. "And you need to stay in bed!"

"It's just fluids," she retorts, ripping the IV from her arm and standing. She sways unsteadily.

"And what do you plan to do about it? You can barely stand!" She sinks back down onto the bed.

"That's better," I soothe. "I can't believe it either. But we have to let the police do their job. If Will *did* kill Justin and that girl, then he needs to face the consequences!"

I straighten the scarf around my neck and replace my hat on my head.

I pat Annie's hand. "You poor thing. Look, I'll go. I just wanted you to know that I'm here for you. When you're ready, when you're better, I hope we can try to have some kind of relationship. It may take time, I understand that, but I'm willing to wait as long as it takes."

Annie's hand curls around my wrist in a surprisingly strong

grip. "Help Will," she growls at me fiercely. "That would be a good start."

"They think he killed Justin!" I protest. "Your husband! Don't you want justice?"

"More than you know." Annie releases my wrist and falls back on her pillows. I pull her covers back up just as a nurse enters.

"You rang, sweet pea?" he asks with a Southern lilt, placing a hand on one cocked hip.

I lift an eyebrow in surprise. Annie must have pushed the call button without me noticing.

"Yes," Annie says meekly, holding out her arm. "My IV came undone."

The nurse narrows his eyes. "It most certainly did. Let me fix you right up."

"I think I'd like to sleep now," Annie declares.

"An excellent idea!" the nurse agrees enthusiastically.

"Thank you for coming, Carol," Annie says. "We'll talk soon, okay?"

I feel satisfied. I said my piece and Annie was receptive. I decide not to push my luck; Laura and Santiago are likely to be back any second.

"Of course, darling," I confirm. "You get some rest. I'll see what I can do for Will," I add, eager to keep building the bond between us.

Annie nods gratefully. "You *know* Will. He's not capable."

"But everyone can surprise us, right? I mean I know you've had to swallow some bitter pills about Justin. As have I. But we have to remember the good in him, right? Isn't that our responsibility as the people who loved him best?"

"Right now, this young lady's only responsibility is to take care of herself!" the nurse declares.

"Of course." I kiss Annie on the forehead.

There's a spring in my step as I head out. Santiago had been awful to me, it's true, but clearly Annie feels differently. She couldn't have been sweeter.

The poor girl. First Justin, then Hayley, now this terrible tragedy. Suicide is so selfish, really, and Hugh Hayter's choice of time and place particularly so. Annie's in a club with me now, the society of those touched by multiple, heartbreaking, catastrophic losses.

I see Laura and Santiago coming my way. Laura looks like she's aged ten years, purple patches like bruises under her eyes, her narrow shoulders slumped in defeat. I pull my hat down low and duck into a stairwell to avoid them. No need to complicate things. Not while I'm ahead.

CHAPTER FORTY

ANNIE

The pull of the sedatives they've given me is deliciously seductive, but my mind is racing. Every time I slide toward oblivion, an insistent prick of anxiety jolts me awake. I pretend to be out cold when Mom and Santi come back; it's easier than submitting to their fussing.

Will arrested for Justin's and Hayley's murders.

Impossible. Could Carol be *lying*? But why would she make up such a thing?

Santi and Mom whisper softly, their conversation providing a soothing background, as familiar as childhood.

But images swirl in my mind's eye. Justin's dead, white face on a cold steel table. His live, warm face leaning in to kiss me with hot, urgent breath. Hugh Hayter's exploding head. I moan, and hear the rustle of Mom's clothes as she turns toward me.

"Is she awake? Annie, are you awake?"

I keep my eyes firmly closed.

"I guess not," Mom says. "I hope she sleeps for hours. The last thing she needs is this news about Will."

So. It's true then.

But Will could *never* have killed Justin and Hayley. It makes no sense.

Of course, I thought Justin was a loving, loyal husband. So, Carol is right, people do surprise you.

I'm a broken widow, now, that's what I am. A broken window.

I feel dizzy. Overcome by a deep sadness. A little nauseous. It must be the drugs. One hand strays to my belly, cupping its slight swell.

Justin and I had laughed for hours making up names for our future children. The conversation would always start seriously: *"What do you think of Alexander?"* But then one of us would inevitably counter back with something absurd: *"What do you think of Flowerpot? She'd be the only one in her class!"*

The jokes were never really that funny; the electricity came from the subtext: We'd be having sex, practicing for making little Flowerpot, often within hours, if not minutes, of our banter.

A deep melancholy surrounds my heart. *I'm sorry, Flowerpot, so sorry.*

Something niggles at the back of my brain, practically doing jumping jacks to get my attention. *What is it?*

Carol's face as she told me about Will's arrest. Was there an eagerness in her eyes? A *pleasure*? That would be sick, to wish that your son's best friend killed him!

On the other hand, I know the gaping wound left in me by Justin's death; the need to understand *how* it happened. How that need left me vulnerable and confused and questioning. In need of answers, no matter how ugly.

And of course, Carol doesn't know Will like I do. A wave of sympathy for Carol pulses through me. *The poor lonely woman. I'll be nicer. It'll hit her hard when she has to accept the truth about Justin.*

Santiago's cellphone rings, the distinctive funky growl of War's "Low Rider."

"Shh!" Mom admonishes. "Don't wake her up."

The rustle of Santiago leaving. His faint "Hello" from out in the hallway as the door swings closed behind him.

I feel Mom's cool hand on my forehead. Sleep beckons, so enticing, so inevitable . . .

The sound of the door opening drags me back.

"That was Lizzie," Santiago intones softly. "God bless that girl. She's handling the press and she found Annie a lawyer. A fancy one. And get this. The police carted off half of what was in Annie's house."

Mom's hand leaves my forehead. I imagine it's at her throat.

"Who knows what's on the asshole's computer? In his files? How he might have implicated her. And in god knows what."

Mom sniffs and blows her nose. She must be crying.

"My poor baby" is the last thing I hear before blessed, blessed sleep takes me under.

CHAPTER FORTY-ONE

WILL

The news is playing in the background on the television at the station house when they book me. Hugh Hayter blew his brains out. At Annie's house. Gotta say, I kinda understand the guy's perspective, even if his choice of location was perverse.

I don't mean to be flip, but as I'm photographed and finger-printed, strip-searched and handed orange scrubs, it's challeng-ing to "stay above the fray," as the trendy meditation guru Justin once brought in for a company workshop advised us. *Find your center and stay above the fray.*

My center is liquid. I've never been more scared in my life. One thing they let you know when they put you in jail: *You belong to them.*

At least the news report said no other casualties, which means Annie is all right. I hope to god she wasn't there at all.

I'm finally shoved in a holding cell with four relatively harmless-looking guys, or at least that's what I tell myself. One of them, with long, dirty blond hair and a fixed sneer on his face, swaggers aggressively over toward me.

Something ancient and proud rises in me. The same impulse

that made me fling myself against my father's back when I saw him hit my mother—an instinctive knowledge that something is not right and I have to be strong enough to meet it.

"What did they get you for?" I bluster, inwardly cringing at how cartoonish I sound.

"Aggravated assault," leers Blondie.

"Huh. Yeah. Murder for me. Two counts, maybe three."

"You don't know for sure?" He looms over me; he smells like garlic and sweat and burnt rubber.

"Day's young," I say with a smile and a shrug. "Don't piss me off."

He barks a laugh and returns to his bench. My heart's hammering. I stare at the bare wall opposite me, eyes fixed.

Dying in prison. Blamed and shamed for crimes I didn't commit. *That* is the legacy my best friend left me. The man I thought of as a brother.

Rage stirs from a pit deep inside of me. It festers and foments, curdles and burbles. *I will not let him do this to me. No.*

Justin always used to praise me to the skies: how brilliant I was, how I'd saved his ass in B school and a thousand times since. I'd always thought he was being unnecessarily self-deprecating; I thought of us as equals, more or less. Justin was the leader in the people-skills department, I was the steady hand on the rudder. *A good team, that was how I thought of us.*

But we weren't a team; I was a pawn.

Annie and I have both been searching for answers, but I don't give a shit about understanding anymore. I just want revenge.

CHAPTER FORTY-TWO

CAROL

Grief has discombobulated me. My sleep is disordered; I forget words, or to eat. I suspect it will be like this for quite some time. But with Will in jail and Annie finally starting to open up, it feels like order is being restored to my little corner of the universe. For the first time since I learned of Justin's death, I feel a mild sense of contentment.

I turn my attention to the problem of Laura and Santiago. They can't be allowed to destroy the precious seedling of intimacy I'm nurturing with Annie. Santiago was impossibly rude, but I've no doubt his macho pride will ensure I never get the apology he owes me.

Maybe I can talk to Laura, though. *Mother to mother.* That's an idea. She'll understand. Surely, she wants everyone who loves and supports Annie to rally around her during this difficult time. It's what I would want if Annie had died and Justin was the grieving widower. A loving community of dependable people my child could rely on.

And anyway, Annie's a grown woman. She can make decisions for herself. She doesn't need her parents' approval to spend time with me.

A little giggle escapes me. I feel impudent and girlish. I think about heading down to the beach. Maybe Santa Monica.

The ocean is always so soothing, its very vastness a comfort. And the cluster of high-end hotels that congregate at the end of Pico Boulevard are a good hunting ground for *an encounter*. I think I need one.

As I dress, I decide on a persona. *China,* I decide, for a first name. A little exotic, it'll inevitably lead to a question and we'll be off to the races. *China Hendrix*. I like the sound of that. A little nod to Annie, a way of keeping us connected.

I select a lightweight navy knit dress that shows just how disciplined I am about maintaining my figure.

"Looking good," I murmur at my reflection. But I pull a rectangle of silk from a drawer, sensitive about my neck. I knot it around my throat. It ruins the lines of the dress.

I pull it off. "Lipstick on a pig, girl," I say to my reflection.

What's China's story? I decide to keep it simple and easy. "I'm here from Long Island on vacation," I tell the adorable twenty-something who can't believe this gorgeous MILF is chatting him up at the hotel bar on the beach. "But I come by my name honestly," I say, brushing my breast against his bare forearm as I reach for my drink. "My parents conceived me in Shanghai."

He turns an enchanting shade of pink. The pickings were slim tonight. I'd been here for a couple of hours before he showed up. He's the only promising prospect of the evening and arrived just when I was giving up hope.

"And you?" I ask him. "You visiting or a local?" I prefer the tourists; even in a big city it diminishes the chance of running into someone *after the fact,* so to speak. *Awkward.*

"Visiting. From Oklahoma."

Perfect.

"First time in L.A.?"

"Yeah. It's a crazy place, huh?"

"Oh, you have no idea." I run a finger up the inside of his thigh.

His enchanting pink shade goes scarlet.

"Are you staying in the hotel?" I whisper.

"Uh. Yeah."

"Do you want to go to your room?"

"Uh, sure. I'll get the check."

As he signals for the bartender, I pull out my compact and reapply my lipstick. *You are beautiful. You deserve this. You're allowed a release.*

"Ready?" This beautiful boy-man I've picked up is off his barstool and bouncing on his feet. *An eager beaver. How cute.*

I lick my index finger lasciviously, enjoying the fun. "Let's go."

"Don't you even want to know my name?" My eager beaver suddenly looks anxious.

"Of course I do, sweetheart," I reassure him. *He's even cuter than I thought. Does he think this is the beginning of something?* "Tell me." I lean in and trail kisses from his ears to his lips. Just as I arrive there . . .

"Justin."

I jerk away. My desire evaporates. Any contentment I was feeling along with it.

"No," I retort.

"Yes. I mean, yes, ma'am, it is. My name is Justin." His wide square face is puzzled. "Justin Obermayer."

"I have to go."

He called me "ma'am"! He fucking called me "ma'am." Rage powers through my body. Stumbling away from the bar, I want to cry and shout, beat someone with my fists until they run bloody.

As I run down the beach, rage ebbs and despair takes hold. Loss consumes me like a hungry ghost. I want to crash my car into a brick wall, slit my wrists, take a handful of pills. Sprint into that ocean and let it swallow me whole.

What do I have to live for anyway?

Annie.

I stop running. I have Annie to live for, and through the two of us, Justin, *my Justin,* will live on forever. Adored. Respected. Loved.

CHAPTER FORTY-THREE

ANNIE

Cousin Lizzie's connections apparently extend from Silicon Valley to the oppressively elegant Beverly Hills law office in which I now find myself waiting with Mom. I have ambivalence about using Lizzie's connections. When we were teenagers, Lizzie talked me out of taking Santi's last name, claiming that a white girl taking a Mexican name was cultural appropriation, no matter how much Santi acted like my father. I backed out of the name change without explanation, too ashamed to explain to my mom and Santi. We didn't sort out that mess until years later at a disastrous family Thanksgiving at which the whole story finally came out.

But once again, the Lizzie Morales magic is in play. I googled the lawyer when Lizzie told me about the appointment. She's represented movie stars with drug problems, politicians in bribery scandals, captains of industry caught with their hands in the till. I seem a very pedestrian client for this firm, but apparently Monica Stanton, Esq., owes Lizzie a favor.

Since I was released from the hospital, I've done *a ton* of thinking, puzzling through the facts as I know them. I feel oddly dispassionate, removed from my hurt and pain, almost as though I'm observing my life from the heady distance of a gaudy hot air balloon dancing above the earth.

I have questions, more than I know what to do with. But I also have suspicions. Convictions. Ideas.

I find myself gnawing a cuticle on the edge of my thumb until it bleeds. I suck at the metallic tang.

The lawyer is not at all what I expect. She's warm and funny and a little disheveled, unlike the sleek shark I'd imagined. She's got an unapologetic Boston accent and a hearty bray of a laugh. Next to me, I can *feel* Mom relax, an almost palpable wave of relief at both Monica's demeanor and her competent assessment of the facts as I set them out.

Her questions are sharp and pointed. I do my best to stay logical, organized, and on point. I'd prepped for this, writing out bullet points of the collapse of my life like I used to prepare for a marketing meeting.

There's a knock at the door. It flies open immediately, and Lizzie marches in, trailing Santiago behind her.

"I'm sorry," he says. "I tried to get her to wait."

"Time doesn't wait for Lizzie Morales," Lizzie announces in her usual brash fashion. "Besides, I'm always welcome here, right, Monica?"

Monica blushes and it dawns on me that the favor Monica Stanton, Esq., owes Lizzie might be of a sexual nature.

It turns out Lizzie has a plan. Not a legal strategy, she assures me, that's Monica's department, but a complementary media plan that she's devised to both help protect me and maximize any opportunities that might be *exploitable* given my circumstances.

Even though this same idea had occurred to me before Hugh blew his brains out and Will was arrested, the events of the past few days altered my view on things. I want to clear Will and then get somewhere far, far away from everyone and everything.

Lizzie is outlining the first step of Phase Three when I interrupt.

"Thanks, Lizzie. Really. And you too, Monica. But I can't do all of that. I can't do any of it." My voice shakes, and I curse myself. I wanted to sound *decisive* and *in control* and instead I have the nervous tenor of a teenager caught breaking curfew.

"Of course you can," Lizzie replies briskly. "I'll be by your side every step of the way. You play this right, Annie, and you could be set for life. Free to write whatever you want. Think about that! After what Justin put you through, don't you owe it to yourself to get a little of your own back?"

"My best friend is in *jail*! I owe it to him to help clear his name!"

"Well, that too, of course." Lizzie frowns, perplexed. "I don't see the problem. The two aren't mutually exclusive."

"Still," I continue with more conviction, "Justin exploited me, Will, god knows how many people! Exploiting the situation seems like a sick continuation of the whole disgusting mess."

Lizzie looks at me with pity and I'm reminded again why she irks me. *Supercilious* is the word that comes to mind.

"The 'disgusting mess' will be exploited one way or another. That's already happening," Lizzie asserts. "The question is whether you want to be controlling the narrative or reacting to it. I'd argue that getting ahead of it is the most powerful thing you can do to take control back. You've been a victim, Annie, but you don't need to stay one."

"Lizzie's plan dovetails with our legal strategy," Monica adds. "This is the best path to realizing all of your agendas."

"Mom?" I turn to her and find her hand at her throat (no surprise there, if she played poker it would be her tell every time).

"I just want Annie to be safe?" It's a question, not a statement. "Will she be safe if we do all you say? Who's to say another Hugh Hayter won't come out of the woodwork? We don't know what other damage that maniac left behind!"

Monica takes this one. "I do suggest staying in a hotel for the time being, instead of going home."

"Like we'd ever go back to that house!" Santi explodes.

I suffer a flash of memory: Hugh's brain matter on my sunny yellow kitchen wall.

"Shh, honey." Mom takes Santi's hand. "Of course not." She turns to Monica. "Our place isn't good enough?"

"It's too easy a target for the paps," Lizzie asserts.

"My office has a list of hotels where we have arrangements for discretion. We'll email you the list," Monica offers.

Everyone is staring at me, waiting for something. An agreement? A media ready smile? I can't remember the last time I smiled.

I recall the night Justin went missing. We'd had a stupid fight. He was mere weeks from the professional milestone he'd worked toward for years. I understood that, but was feeling lonely and abandoned, and he had nothing to give. Both of us had said things we'd regretted. At least I know I did. He went out to "clear his head."

Three hours later, I called Carol, who sounded surprised and pleased to hear from me, but when she asked if she could speak to Justin. I lied and said he was snoring on the sofa in front of the TV.

But her question answered mine: Justin hadn't gone to see his mother.

The hours drew later; it became too late to check with Will or any of Justin's other friends. I thought about calling Bella, but I felt uneasy about revealing trouble in paradise to her scrutiny.

As dawn approached, I spiraled. My inner voices were screaming at me: *Of course he left you, you pathetic, stupid fool. Everyone leaves you.*

I calculated the time difference and tried Mom overseas but the call went to voicemail. *What is she going to do from Hong Kong anyway?* I wondered as I heaped a fresh round of emotional abuse on myself.

When the doorbell rang, I was haggard, fragile, terrified. Also praying it was Justin, sheepish and loving. He'd lost his keys, been mugged, couldn't call. I swore I would allow relief to temper rage and just be grateful to see him. We'd take this dreadful, petty moment and direct our marriage back to the right track.

It was the police. They confirmed my identity and my relationship to Justin. Regretfully informed me. And told me they needed me to come identify his body.

I realize I've gnawed my thumb's cuticle raw. It stings and pulses and I clasp my hands together in my lap. "Okay," I say. "I'll follow the script."

Lizzie's right. It's time for me to write my own story.

CHAPTER FORTY-FOUR

WILL

Getting locked up was never among my ambitions. But it's where they've led me. And it's pretty fucking grim: gray and hard-edged, and I'm referring to the people as well as the environment.

But it's left me loads of time to think.

Best as I can figure, "our resident genius" turned out to be less of a genius than advertised and Justin talked Hayley into "sharing" proprietary haptic tech MediFutur had developed for training surgeons.

Why did Justin kill her? A mystery to me. Something went wrong, obviously.

And here's another question I'm toying with, now that I have time on my hands: I know I didn't kill Justin. So how did he die? Did he kill himself? Was he suicidal because of whatever had "gone wrong" with Hayley?

I could kick myself. I'm sitting in a cell because of that motherfucker and still trying to find evidence of his conscience!

If he had one.

There were clues in front of me all along, I realize, if only I'd been bothering to look. Like if there was no Thomas Childs, the entire Thomas Childs Memorial Fund for Addiction Research, for which Justin had quietly raised money for years, was no doubt also fraudulent.

I never questioned the legitimacy of the fund, but why would I? We both ran 5Ks and raised money for the charity, and the more Justin asked me to play it down, citing a combination of modesty about his good works and a little shame about Tommy's "weakness," the more I quietly asked people to support it.

There were so many things I accepted at face value: Justin's pedigree, the terms of my investment in Convincer, his steady hand on the financial till, his seemingly genuine affection *for* me, and reliance *on* me.

You were good, my former friend, you were in your own way quite brilliant.

An odd kind of peace settles within me with that mental tip of the hat.

But the question still remains. Was Justin's death an accident as the police initially suspected before my current nightmare? A combination of drugs and an unfortunately sharp curve? Or was he murdered? Did *someone* kill him?

The irony strikes me. The Justin that I knew and loved was generous with his own time and money to excess. As a consequence, he made friends everywhere. But the other Justin, the liar I now know him to be, was quietly and secretly accumulating god knows how many enemies.

I wonder why Sunil hasn't been to see me. Even if he hasn't found a magic bullet to get me out of this, he could at least give me a progress report.

My heart's beating a mile a minute. For the very first time

since the cops showed up at the Convincer office, I believe, truly believe, that I might in fact go to prison for life. Or worse.

When I hear the guard call "Barber," it takes a moment for my name to register. Then I spring to my feet, desperate to escape this holding cell populated by dark souls and the acrid scent of desperation. I realize the scent is my own.

"Me!" I yell absurdly, like a child volunteering to write on a blackboard. "That's me," I repeat more softly.

"You've made bail."

Thank god.

Each step of my release is agonizingly slow, from the opening of the cell to the return of my belongings.

When the last door slides open, I step through with an audible sigh.

Waiting for me is Annie, flanked by her parents and her cousin Lizzie. With them is a dumpy middle-aged woman, clad in a suit and carrying a briefcase, who I deduce is my new representation. She looks about as threatening as a baby bunny, not the firepower I expect I'm going to need.

"Monica Stanton," she introduces herself, shaking my hand with a surprisingly strong grip.

"Oh!" The startled exclamation bursts from my lips and Stanton gives me an amused and knowing glance.

Even I know Monica Stanton's name and reputation. She's a killer, exactly who I need.

Just proving, once again, that looks can be deceiving.

CHAPTER FORTY-FIVE

CAROL

I once read a magazine article about a woman in the middle of a divorce who spied on her cheating husband for days on end by camping out in her car with supplies of bottled water, beef jerky, and Depends. The last is starting to feel like a good idea. I've been in my car waiting for over two hours now.

Finally. There he is, Will, blinking in the sun. He's with Annie, her parents, and a couple of women I'm not sure I can place. Santiago glances in my direction and I slide lower in my seat, glad I've taken the precaution of a nondescript rental. I suspected Annie would get involved with Will's release and I need to stay in the shadows if I am to protect her.

The group splits up. The two women depart in a Porsche Cayenne. Definitely not from the public defender's office then. *Lucky you, Will. That Annie is a loyal girl. She must have hooked you up with someone powerful.*

I expected Will would get released in twenty-four hours. From what I understand, the evidence against him for Justin's murder is circumstantial and the financial crimes at Convincer are right now a hornet's nest of confusion and accusations.

I sigh. Determining *the truth* is so complicated these days. The deliberate obfuscation is keeping him out of jail. For now.

Laura and Santiago take off in Laura's Subaru wagon. Annie and Will embrace.

They remain intertwined and rigidly still for so long it makes me uncomfortable. Then a subtle tremble shakes the interlocked pair from head to toe. Will's *crying*. Holding it back as best he can, but wracked with sobs. He and Annie cling to each other for dear life. I have to look away, it feels *dirty* to watch them.

A gut-hollowing cloud of loneliness descends over me, so pervasive and powerful it leaves me cringing. My palms sweat against the steering wheel. I pull the car's visor down and stare at my reflection in its little mirror, hoping to reassure myself that yes, I'm still here. Still alive on this earth. Still thinking, doing, *feeling*.

The mirror's too small for me to see my whole image, so I examine myself in fragments. My makeup is perfectly applied. This was something my mother taught me before she died: A lady never goes outside without her "face on." (I must have been only three years old the first time I remember her saying that. It could be my earliest memory. I was confounded and afraid: Did this mean she might *take her face off* once we were back inside our house?)

A silk scarf hides the worst of my neck. A cold-shoulder style sweater accentuates the blessedly still smooth skin on the tops of my shoulders. But with all the effort I've made, I still find countless flaws.

I have three hairs sprouting on my chin. Two are brown; one is long and gray and wiry. I long for a tweezer even though I know I don't have one on me. A dusting of brown spots has erupted near my hairline. I would like to pretend they are freckles born from my new life in the Southern California sun, but I know they are age spots. The thin skin above my upper lip shows a faint pucker, a telltale sign of worse to follow.

I snap the visor shut. No point in dwelling on what can't be changed. If life has taught me one thing, that would be it. You are where you are. And the sooner any person accepts reality and examines the facts squarely instead of pretending to themselves, or wishing things were different, the sooner that person can actually let go of the past, make a change, and move on.

The pretenders and the wishers stay stuck, for the simple fact that deep down they are happy with whatever sick or twisted status quo they've convinced themselves they need. Codependency. The shrink I saw after Justin went away to college taught me about that.

Will and Annie are in her car now, and I follow them, trying to keep a few cars back. I rehearse what I'll say if they catch me: *"What a crazy coincidence, but I'm so happy to see you both!"*

I also suspect I may be paranoid; surely Annie and Will aren't peering around corners to see if they're being followed! They have enough on their plates.

Either way, I hold Will responsible for my son's death. He

may have fooled Justin once, Annie, and me too, for that matter, but now that I know who he truly is, I can only admire Justin more.

And look how that was repaid! Will Barber deserves no mercy.

All that fake bullshit Will spouted at Justin's funeral when he had been the very one to stab Justin in the back!

And in the heart too, it appears, I note wryly as I watch Will run long fingers through Annie's hair.

It's hard for any parent to see a child's flaws, or "stretches," as they used to say at Justin's progressive preschool. It's one reason why mental illness goes untreated or drug addictions unseen until the victim is too far gone to save. No one is handed a manual when they have a kid; we all just make it up as we go along and hope for the best.

But a mother knows her son, and I knew my son better than most. He was capable of the *expedient lie* certainly, and I'm not particularly proud he had that propensity, but a ruthless killer he *was not*. I know Will Barber is at the heart of this bloody mess.

The urgency to protect and connect with Annie burns hotly inside me. Justin was the apple of my eye, of course, but I often wished for a daughter. Someone to shop and gossip with, someone with whom I could commiserate about the many indignities of being female in this man's world. No matter how close Justin and I were, we never could have had that kind of relationship.

When it becomes apparent that Annie's heading to Will's place, I stop following them and take a different route. I'll show up there before them, I bet, if I use the shortcut Justin showed me on Rose. Better yet, I'll find a coffee place and use the bathroom, get something to drink, check my makeup.

Offering up a silent prayer to my son, I promise him that justice will be done. Will Barber may be a conniving, murderous son of a bitch, but he won't get away with it. And he won't get Annie in the end, not if I have anything to say about it.

CHAPTER FORTY-SIX

ANNIE

Will's apartment near the beach has always felt comfortable and homey to me. As long as I've known him, he's said he plans to move "this year." Somehow it never happens. But I think the place suits him. It's small and spare and organized. The sound of the ocean is a constant, soothing background soundtrack. Will spends much of his time on the terrace, which provides a view spectacular enough to compensate for the cramped living space.

Will's showering. I'm making us some tea.

I grab a bottle of scotch from his rolling bar cart. I'm my mother's daughter, after all; a shot for "medicinal purposes" has never seemed more appropriate.

Will comes back in clean and changed, damp strands of hair clinging to his neck. His eyes have a haunted quality; I hope it's just exhaustion.

We sit outside on the terrace. We drink tea with healthy dollops of scotch and share a package of Nilla Wafers I found in a cupboard. We compare notes and trade information, bringing each other up to speed about Justin's many, many lies and transgressions we've unearthed. Will also shares what Monica's learned the police have in evidence against him. It's largely circumstantial, but includes an email from Justin that Molly received posthumously, and another Justin sent to Carol accusing Will of embezzlement and expressing fear for his life.

"Well," I say finally. "I'm kind of speechless."

"Yeah," Will agrees. "It's a lot to take in. Listen, Annie . . ." He trails off.

"Go on. Spit it out."

"Thanks for Monica Stanton. You have no idea . . ."

"Aw shucks, Barber, you would have done the same for me." Will stares so deeply into my eyes that I feel a blush start to rise from my chest.

There's a charged moment between us. Magnetic. As in having the quality of magnetism.

> **magnetism** [ˈmag-nə-ˌti-zəm]
>   *noun,* a physical phenomenon produced by the motion of electric charge, resulting in attractive and repulsive forces between objects

Never has a classic definition been so apt. This feels good. This feels awful. This *definitely* feels weird. I get up and go inside on the pretext of wanting more scotch. Maybe it's not a pretext. I pour a healthy slug into my mug.

I pause for a minute next to six small square framed drawings mounted on the wall. They are a set of cocktail napkins on which Will and Justin scribbled sample logos for Convincer, the sixth and final drawing being a close approximation of the ultimate choice.

When I go back out to the terrace, Will's standing, leaning

on the railing, staring out at the beige sand below and the gray-blue Pacific beyond. A seagull aggressively attacks a fast-food wrapper down on the beach, wheeling about and squawking in an unseemly manner.

"I'm sorry," Will says without meeting my eyes.

"You have nothing to be sorry about," I reply lightly.

"Annie." Will turns to me and brings soulful eyes to meet mine. He takes both my hands between his larger ones.

"No, Will," I implore, extricating my hands from his. "Don't."

I'm grieving and confused and full of regrets. The last thing I want is another one.

"All right. Let me just say this, though. When I saw on the news what Hugh had done, when I thought you might have been hurt . . . or worse . . . I can't stand the idea of losing you. So, whatever it looks like, just . . . be with me. Here. Now."

Will enfolds me in a hug. I surrender to it. He's warm and solid and smells like Ivory soap. I'd like to stay in his embrace all day, but it's confusing the hell out of me. I pull away, plop back down in one of the terrace's two chairs, and shake another cookie loose from the packet.

Will pulls his phone from his pants pocket. "It's my mother," he says with some dread in his voice as he looks at the screen. "I'd better get this over with."

He answers his cell and steps inside to take the call.

The waves beat against the sand with their rhythmic insistence. Surfers fall and rise in the water. Three wild parrots fly by, a little close for comfort. They alight on the next terrace and one of them tilts its emerald green head at me.

"*You're a loser,*" the bird lectures me. "*Loser. Fuck you.*"

Thanks for the support, I think wryly.

The trio takes flight again, their bright feathers in sharp relief against the brilliant blue sky.

Piecing Justin together is like trying to coax a clear image from a kaleidoscope. The pieces keep turning and falling as my eyes strain to make sense of the jumble. There is the *story* he presented, the lies we've uncovered, the version Carol sees, some version of a truth that contains elements of all.

The resolve that took root in Monica Stanton's elegant Beverly Hills office settles into my core. Justin Childs, my *beloved* husband, took a *wrecking ball* to my life. I can't sit back and just watch it crumble.

I sift and sort through what I know. Justin lied recklessly, expeditiously, relentlessly. Yet he was able to manipulate us all, even from the grave! I shake my head thinking about Molly, how easily she turned on Will, how willing she was to believe the worst of him.

Will's confession of feelings for me pricks uncomfortably. Maybe Molly was so quick to believe Justin's email because she sensed an underlying truth, at least in how he feels about me.

Did Justin fool Carol too? I wonder. She worshipped the ground he walked on, but how much did she know about his true nature? About how terribly her beloved son has betrayed me and Will?

I pull over the legal pad with the timeline of lies Will and I constructed; all of Justin's (known) falsehoods listed on one side, truths (as we now know them) lined up opposite. I study the pages. There's still a raft of blanks and question marks.

I study the puzzle that is my husband's real and manufactured life. Questions lead to speculations, then turn into suspicions.

With a blossoming sense of hope, I am virtually certain I know exactly what happened. And how to prove it.

It dawns on me that maybe I am Justin's equal, after all. Fuck that, I'm his *better*.

A smile, an honest-to-god real smile, tugs at my lips.

CHAPTER FORTY-SEVEN

WILL

This outdoor bar is one of my favorite haunts in Venice. It's perched on a rooftop right above the strand, making creative and somewhat awkward use of what an old building had to offer when a hipster hotel chain took over the site.

The hotel's only ten stories high, but everything else along the beach is low, so the ocean views are spectacular. The Santa Monica Pier amusement park is visible to the north, the neon lights of the Ferris wheel winking electric color against the night sky.

Pyramidal heat lamps flare more for atmosphere than warmth around groupings of couches and low tables. The crowd in the bar is lively, fashionable. Laughter bubbles, the occasional shout or groan pops the buzz of conversation. I'm reminded that other people's lives are not a shit show.

Did I mention I've had a couple of martinis?

I order another one at the standing-room-only bar.

"They were my father's special-occasion cocktail," I tell the bartender. "Birthdays, anniversaries, Christmas."

"To your father," he replies convivially as he pours icy liquid from a shaker into a glass.

"He died yesterday."

The bartender plops two olives into my drink. "Sorry to hear it, man. This one's on the house. Was it sudden?"

"Yeah. He heard I got arrested for murder and had a heart attack."

The bartender stops moving for the first time since I've seen him tonight. He looks at me intently, trying to gauge if I'm full of shit.

"Yeah," I continue. "No lie. His wife, Brandy, she said they did their best, but he died in the ambulance on the way to the hospital. She's a fucking child, by the way, younger than I am. At least he died a happy man."

I raise my martini glass skyward in a toast to my father, then drain it.

"One more, my good man!" I slam the glass down on the bar, but the bartender has moved on, whirring a blender down the bar.

This time, the pretty tattooed bartender serves me. She's fucking gorgeous; I wonder why she shaves off her hair. Is it *because* she's so beautiful? The red light above the bar glints off her shiny skull. The tattoo above her left ear reads DEMON CHILD.

I wander over to the railing at the western end of the bar, my legs surprisingly rubbery. That's what three martinis will do to you. *Or was it four?*

Random snippets of conversation drift over to me:

"A fucking unitard! I kid you not!"

"No, I think she's his fifth wife. What about that Brazilian girl? Wasn't he married to her?"

"And then I told him to take his blueprints and shove them up his bleached asshole!"

Maybe other people's lives *are* a shit show, after all.

I think about Annie. About her pulling away when I tried to get real about my feelings.

I remember how I felt the day Justin proposed to her. I was in on it, of course, Justin's trusty lieutenant. The whole elaborate setup at the hotel downtown. Inviting our friends. Flying in Justin's mother from New York. Arranging for that ridiculous slide.

Just for the record, I argued against that stupid idea. I told him the proposal would be worthless if Annie had a heart attack (*irony alert*), but Justin was adamant.

For the first time since that day, I'm squarely honest with myself about the small quiver of loss I felt when Annie said "yes" to Justin. I buried it then. Of course I did. They were the two people I loved best in the world. Why would I ever do anything to fuck that up?

If I knew then . . .

People blather on about the benefits of hindsight, how lessons learned inform the future, why we need to pick ourselves up and learn from our mistakes. *Fuck that shit.*

I thought Justin was one of the great miracles of my life, but he was a *curse.* I'm glad he's dead. But what has he left for me in this life? Convincer's going down, my foreseeable future is all lawyers and the media circus.

I sip my tangy drink, I sway out over the railing, leaning as far as I dare, tempting gravity.

"You okay there?" A tall, skinny dude in a porkpie hat grips my arm, his eyebrows knitted together in concern.

"I'll never make it right with my father," I tell this kind

stranger. "He'll never get his chance for a fatherhood do-over. And my twin half-sisters? They're just little kids. They'll grow up without any father at all. I even feel bad for Brandy! Even if she is kind of a slut."

"Right," Porkpie says uncertainly. "Are you here with anyone? Maybe you should call an Uber."

"Fuck you, Justin Childs."

Wow. That felt great. I say it again, this time with loud and conscious conviction: "Fuck you, Justin Childs." I drain my glass and smash it on the ground.

The surrounding strangers glance over at me in surprise. Some alarm. I ignore them.

Pulling away from Porkpie, I spring up onto the railing that rims the western edge of the roof and crouch there, clinging to the spiky metal, peering down. No inflatable slide this time.

Gasps fill the air. I sense, rather than see, people pulling out their cellphones and filming me.

Porkpie pulls me back onto the roof almost instantly. We tumble backward and land hard as the crowd around us scatters and shrieks.

"I've got you," Porkpie murmurs in my ear.

"Enough!" I exclaim, pulling away from him. "You should have let me die! I admit it, I killed him! He was fucking me over in every possible way and I killed him!"

"Whoa!" Porkpie raises his palms in supplication. "What the hell are you talking about?"

"I'm confessing to murder. The murder of Justin Childs. He deserved it, the motherfucker, and I'm not sorry." A sea of cellphones surrounds me, recording my every word.

Porkpie backs away from me. "Okay, man, not really my

problem. I just came for the view. Stay safe, okay?" He backs away and disappears from my sight.

Whispers ricochet through the crowd. I hear snippets: *Can you freaking believe that? I wonder what TMZ'll pay for the video? That gorgeous guy who crashed his car, that's who. Did somebody call the police?*

I stay where I am, sitting cross-legged on the sticky floor, until I'm arrested again.

CHAPTER FORTY-EIGHT

CAROL

When Annie invited me for dinner, just the two of us, I was elated.

Will's still maintaining that Justin was responsible for the Ponzi scheme that is Convincer and for killing Hayley Hayter, but why should any of us believe an admitted murderer? I'm practically giddy about the closure finally being granted to Annie and me.

I've taken even more care than usual getting dressed today. The lilac cashmere I'm wearing complements my coloring and I've coordinated my jewelry carefully, an amethyst necklace around my neck and matching earrings on my lobes.

Annie suggested the elegant restaurant in the courtyard of the Hammer Museum, walking distance from my apartment. It's a lovely spot, with expensive food as artistic as the works the museum houses. It's a splurge on my budget, but it's a special occasion I hope, the beginning of new era for me and Annie.

I arrive fifteen minutes early so I can slip my credit card to the waiter. I don't want any awkward fumbling for the check. This will be my treat.

To my surprise, Annie is already there, seated at a table, sipping an iced tea. She waves and rises when she sees me.

"Hi, Carol," she greets me. "You look wonderful! That's such a good color on you."

"Thank you, sweetheart. You're looking well yourself." Annie does look well. A healthy flush back in her cheeks, her hair carefully groomed. She's wearing a bold red lipstick that makes her mouth pop.

"You're early," I say, taking my seat.

Annie waves her hand airily. "I left when I was dressed and ready. Weird to have no schedule." She giggles nervously and it occurs to me that maybe she isn't drinking iced tea, after all. "Anyway, here we are. What would you like to drink?" she asks me as our waiter materializes.

"What are you having?"

"Iced tea. And I'll have another, thanks." She slurps at her eco-friendly metal straw until the glass is empty but for melting ice cubes. Her behavior makes me suspect she really arrived early to make some private arrangement with the waiter—*iced tea* being code for something less benign.

"The same," I order, a little touched by her anxiety. *This is as important to her as it is to me.*

We take care of the rituals. Unfold our napkins and put them on our laps. Decide what to order. Debate the chocolate soufflé special that requires ordering in advance of the meal. Impulsively, I agree to it, with extra whipped cream on the side. It's a celebration, after all.

As we eat, we tentatively wade into the news of Will's confession. We're just finishing our entrée and I'm treading carefully into the question of his culpability in Convincer's collapse, when Annie lays a gentle hand over mine.

"I have a question for you," Annie says. "And I need you to be honest with your answer. Because I really want us to have a relationship."

"Of course, honey," I assure her. My heart swells.

"Did you tip the police off about Will?"

"Will *confessed*."

"I know. I saw the video along with half of America. But that doesn't answer my question. Did you have evidence implicating Will in Justin's death that you took to the police?"

I sip at my champagne, uncertain how to answer. Will's confession is the thing that will cinch his conviction. Whether I shared anything else with the police hardly seems relevant.

Annie slumps back in her seat. Lifts her hand away from mine. I feel its absence like a cold shadow. She frowns.

"I'm sorry, Carol. But Will's lawyer, well, she says you did. That you forwarded an email Justin sent you. It's in evidence. You may think you're sparing me, because you know I care about Will, but I want to put Justin's killer behind bars as much as you, maybe more . . ." Annie's eyes leak tears. She blows her nose into her napkin before continuing.

"It'll all come out at Will's trial anyway. But more important, if you and I are to be a family, we need total honesty between us. I've had enough lies! I need the truth from here on out. I can't do this any other way."

"Do what?" With the pads of my fingertips I smooth the furrow that's formed in my forehead. *Don't want to get wrinkles.*

Annie lays her palm across her stomach. Takes a deep

breath. "I'm pregnant, Carol. You're going to be a grand-mother."

My heart stops. The room spins, then carousels to a halt. I'm on my feet. Annie's on hers. We're hugging. I'm crying. *A baby.*

The waiter arrives with our soufflé. I order two glasses of champagne. Annie protests. I tell her she'll just have a sip.

"Oh my god," I babble as we take our seats. "When are you due? How do you feel? Who's your obstetrician?"

Annie laughs. "First answer my question, Carol. This child I'm carrying? He, or she, has the right to know everything about how Justin died and about how his killer was brought to justice."

I sip at my champagne. Look at Annie's flat belly and imagine the child growing within her. Justin's child. My second chance.

Annie continues, a solemn look on her face. "This baby will allow Justin to live on for both of us. It's a miracle really. Like a divine intervention that brought him back to us."

It's as if she's saying the very things I'm thinking! A sense of true happiness settles over me, rare and pure.

"And this baby will be special, just like Justin was special. Just like you are, Carol. I'm sorry if I haven't told you that enough."

"You're right," I admit. "Yes. I gave the police an email Justin sent to me."

I clear my throat and gather strength as I continue. "When I got it, he was already dead! I thought it was some sick prank, and I was just going to trash it. But some instinct told me to hang on to it. So I did. Did you know you can schedule an email to be sent anytime you want? I feel a little silly that I hadn't known that, actually. Remember how Justin used to tease me about how the simplest tech confounded me?"

"Of course. His soliloquy on your love/hate relationship with your universal remote? A classic."

We share a warm smile.

I finish my champagne and start on Annie's. "Before he died, Justin was worried. He said some things to me alluding to wrongdoing on Will's part, but he was always vague. When I asked questions, he shut me out, said it would be better if I didn't know the details."

Annie nods. "He always was so protective of you. It was one of the first things I liked about him."

I pat her hand, grateful for the comment. "Then I got that email."

"What did it say exactly?" Annie presses.

"That Justin was scared. That he'd confronted Will and it hadn't gone well. He wanted to give Will a chance to fix things, but, well, Will got violent. Justin was planning on going to the police. He wanted me to know in case something happened to him."

"Oh my god! You poor thing. What a shock that must have been."

We sit in silence for a moment. The waiter approaches and we both wave him away before I continue. "He also told me that he loved me. And you, Annie. If anything happened to him, he wanted us both to know that."

I drain the last of the celebratory champagne. Annie sips at her iced tea.

"You want to watch the iced tea," I say kindly. "Too much caffeine isn't good for the baby."

"But you wrote that email, right, Carol?" Annie's tone is mild, her eyes wide and innocent.

"What? No. Of course not."

Annie leans in so our faces are mere inches apart. "Just like you wrote the one to Molly accusing Will of sleeping with me and embezzling from the company."

A hot flush sweeps through me. Sweat drips between my breasts, down the back of my neck. I press a cool champagne glass to my forehead. "Hot flash," I say, with the most casual laugh I can muster. "Just awful."

"Is that what it is?" Annie continues sweetly. "Or is it something else? Guilty conscience, maybe?"

"Why are you doing this? Will *confessed*."

Annie shrugs, an eloquent expression of sadness. "I know. I'm shocked. Heartbroken. Sick of being lied to! That's why I need complete honesty between us if you want to be in the baby's life."

Of course I want to be in the baby's life. I scoop up the last of the whipped cream and swallow it down.

"I think I understand, Carol. I really do. You suspected Will when Justin died. When you learned about the embezzlement and Hayley, you wanted to be certain Will was convicted."

I lay down my spoon. "Like I said, Justin had already alluded to trouble at Convincer and also to some questionable behavior on Will's part. Something about signing Justin's name to a check. Credit cards he hadn't known about. Anyway, that was the gist of it. Then Justin ended up in a ditch." My next words are pure acid. "So yes, I sent those emails. I only repeated what Justin had told me! Will Barber should pay for destroying Justin's life."

"Oh, I think Justin destroyed his own life."

"He didn't! He was a victim!"

"I wish I could see it that way, Carol, I really do. But he screwed me financially too, you know, me and the baby. I don't own our house! I could be homeless!"

"Never. You'll always have a place with me. Always!"

"Thank you," Annie says, dabbing at her eyes. "I appreciate that. But you see that makes it even more imperative. We must have total honesty between us if we are going to raise the baby together."

Annie reaches for my hand and places it on her stomach. I know it's impossible this early on, but I swear I feel the flutter of new life.

"Look, Carol," she says in a voice like silk. "I know now what Justin was. It's okay. I love him anyway. Just the way you and I will love his child. Unconditional, right? Isn't that what parental love is all about?"

"You're right," I agree fervently. "You'll see when the baby comes, everything shifts, you'll do *anything* for your child."

"Tell me what you did for Justin."

"I told you. I sent those emails."

"That's not all though, right? It's just you and me and little Sparky here—that's what I'm calling the fetus—just the family. Tell me. No judgment."

I look into Annie's clear eyes. She's smiling, nodding, welcoming.

"Justin wasn't like other people." I pause.

"I knew that much the first time I met him. Go on."

"He was brilliant! Spectacular. *You* know." I drop my voice down a notch. "But he made mistakes."

"We all do," Annie chimes in encouragingly.

"But Hayley. He . . . he came to see me. Told me that she'd caught Will stealing something from MediFutur and was going to the police. That they'd argued; Justin wanted to talk to Will first and give him a chance to clear his name."

"And then what happened?"

"Promise me, you'll never say a word. This is our secret. To the grave."

"To the grave," Annie repeats.

"It was an accident! Hayley and Justin were fighting and she fell and cracked her head on the coffee table. Then he panicked. And it was all Will's fault, really!" There's a relief in saying the words, but also a deep sense of unreality. These harsh truths seem out of place in this genteel setting, outrageous when heard out loud.

"Thank you, Carol."

The waiter brings the check. Annie asks for some water.

"Good girl," I compliment her. "It's very important to hydrate."

"There's just one last thing," Annie says, leaning her elbows on the table. "Why did Justin die?"

"You know why he died. He was in a car accident."

"Right. But is it just a coincidence that there are so many car accidents in our family? Your husband died in one. It's how I met Justin. And it's how we lost him." Annie's eyes bore into mine. "Like I said, no judgment. We're just building a bridge of trust."

I imagine Annie and my grandchild livening up my rectangular box of an apartment. I pull out my compact and freshen my lipstick. The tissue-paper-thin folds along my upper lip remind me of my inevitable ruin. But Justin, my beautiful son, he'll remain preserved forever. Young, handsome, perfect. And his child will grow up in my home.

"He'd killed someone, you understand," I murmur.

Annie nods, compassion in her eyes. I feel almost hypnotized, compelled to tell her.

"And even with an accidental death, he'd probably go to jail, he'd have been branded. His life would have been in ruins." I stop.

"My life too," Annie adds. "I thought it *was* actually. Until the doctor told me at the hospital. This baby is giving me new hope. For the family we'll make."

"I fed Justin the Valium without him knowing." *There. I've said it.*

Annie gasps. Jerks away from me. I grip her forearm to pull her back close. I know when I explain it all, she'll understand.

"You were the one who wanted complete honesty! And you'll understand, now that you're going to be a mother! The world couldn't know Justin as a killer! My sweet, lovely boy. It was better that he die with his reputation unblemished than live with that."

Annie crosses her arms over her chest. I realize she's shaking uncontrollably. "Are you all right?" I ask, alarmed. "What's happening? Is the baby okay?"

"You killed him. Your own son."

"I *saved* him. You have to look at it that way. It's the same reason I framed Will. To protect Justin! And it was all Will's fault really! He was an embezzler. Justin, my poor boy, was only trying to protect him. It's poetic justice that Will confessed. He knows in his heart that he's responsible. Surely you understand."

"No, I don't." Annie rises. "Thank god I don't. And I never will."

I'm desperate for her to stay. I grab her wrist and grip it tightly. "He'd killed someone! And I saw it in his eyes! He'd gotten a taste for it. How long could I protect his reputation? I knew he would kill again! I had to stop him in order to save him."

"And you, Carol?" Annie's eyes blaze into mine. "Have you gotten a taste for it?"

She wrenches her arm from my grip and turns to the diners at the table next to us. "Did you get all that?" she asks. "Fucking monster," she mutters at me before spinning away.

I call after her, but suddenly my arms are pinned.

I'm arrested, my rights read. "It'll be Justin's baby. You can't escape that!" I shout. "You'll look at that child every day and wonder if he'll have a taste for it too! Then you'll see! Then you'll understand what a mother will do for her child!"

Annie turns to face me.

"About that, Carol," she announces. "I'm not pregnant. Never have been. A blessing considering the lineage."

My body sags against my captors. My fight is gone.

"And oh, one other thing. Will recanted. Just as soon as we were sure you'd have seen his performance, along with the rest of the world."

My hands are cuffed. Annie walks out and a sense of inevitability overwhelms me.

This is what I deserve.

Because I'll admit another truth. When I snuck out that fateful night my family died, I saw a candle tip over. It fell over in the attic bedroom I shared with my sister as I climbed out the window to meet Bobby Tanaka. I hesitated, but I was already barely clinging to the slippery edge of the roof, about to drop down to the ground. And so I did, with only a quick final glance back at the house before I sped away into the dark night dreaming only of kisses.

I told myself I wasn't really sure if the candle had fallen over, that if it had, the flame had surely guttered out, and that if it hadn't, my sister was certain to wake up and put it out before anything *serious* happened.

That was the lie I told myself. Because Susan was in the habit of slipping a little scotch into her tea from the bottle our mother kept in the kitchen for "special occasions." It was Susan's little act of rebellion, drinking under their own roof while my parents were obliviously charmed by her sudden interest in tea varieties and brewing methods.

But Susan wasn't so understanding of my own rebellion. She didn't approve of Bobby Tanaka, older than I, and with a reputation as a bit of a player. The last thing I wanted was her interference with my plans, so as we finished dinner, I offered to brew her evening tea, with a little wink that let her know I was in on her game. I added the Benadryl along with the scotch.

If a candle did fall in our bedroom that night, there was no way Susan would have woken up, but all these years later, the truth is still a twisted knot. Over the years, my memories became spotty, unreliable, reshaped and honed by shock, time, and desperate need as I endlessly revisited the tragedy in my mind.

I tortured myself. Years later, the memory shifted. I told myself I'd *invented* a memory of the candle falling as a way of overcoming my survivor's guilt. And all these years later, who really knows?

But in my heart I know. I killed my entire family. They burned to death for the sake of a kiss from a boy who never even spoke to me again after the tragedy.

Is it any wonder I'm being punished?

ANNIE

Once Carol started talking, she continued, in her affable, reasonable way. She confessed not only to drugging Justin but to sending him on an errand on a route that she knew would take him to a construction-riddled, already dangerous section of Mulholland Drive.

When asked what she would have done if he hadn't died that night, she shrugged and said she would have tried again.

When asked why she thought Will confessed to Justin's death, she replied that she believed Will was the real criminal trying to smear Justin's name, so she thought divine justice was at work.

Clearly, she's as bat-shit crazy as her son.

A neighbor of Justin's at the Windjammer apartment came forward. She'd heard Justin and Hayley fighting the day he killed her. It seems Hayley's conscience was bothering her and she was going to tell her employers that she had given Justin stolen tech. It turned out to be the proprietary haptic technology from MediFutur's surgery training initiative, the very program that had absorbed my work life for the last year.

We may never know for sure, but I suspect Hayley's death was no accident, despite what Justin may have told Carol. Or maybe Carol lied about that too.

I've resolved to look forward, not back. Trying to unravel Justin's every lie and manipulation was a fall into quicksand— tempting to succumb to, but ultimately suffocating. I'm pulling myself free, but it hasn't been easy.

After Carol's arrest, I stayed with Mom and Santi for a couple of weeks. They were wonderful, but tiptoed around me like I might shatter. Their very *kindness* was an irritant, so I moved to Bella's. But she and her new stuntman boyfriend are turning into a thing (despite my cynicism), and I found all that gooey-eyed young love a bit too much to bear right now.

Lately I've been staying at Will's. He's sleeping on the sofa and has given me his bedroom. We take long walks on the beach every morning, trying to exorcize the past and make some sense of the future. We both want to look forward, but staying firmly in the present is a necessary first step.

On our way back from trudging through the sand, sweaty and sticky with sunscreen, we stop at a local grocery store and buy just enough food for that one day. We shower and change and then cook and eat together, letting the days pass in a blur of comforting, simple routine. I've started writing again. Will's constructing a table out of driftwood. Cinnamon Toast is the third member of our little trio now, happily oblivious to the damage Justin left behind.

I let the banks take the house and I quit my job. Going back seemed untenable, so I resigned before I was fired. With no husband, no money, and no job, my identity is *re-forming* (to put it politely).

Convincer collapsed. The company was a Ponzi scheme of

credit card debt, multiple diverted mortgages (even on Carol's apartment), and a trail of rooked investors Will never even knew about.

Will's in the muck. He'll be cleared of any wrongdoing, but the stench of the scandal will take a long time to fade. He's trying hard to find this new chapter freeing, and to bolster me up, but I see the anxiety that creases his face when he thinks I'm not looking.

Will and I have debated it, why Justin never tried to get me to get him the tech he so desperately sought from MediFutur. Will thinks it was because he was genuinely in love with me.

I'm sorry to say it, but a small piece of me still thrills to that belief. When we were together, I felt chosen, special, infused with a kind of glamour.

glamour [ˈgla-mər]
   noun, 1. an air of compelling charm, romance, and excitement, esp. when delusively alluring; 2. archaic: a magic spell or enchantment

This definition from my favorite childhood dictionary seems particularly apt in the wake of recent events.

Justin was a master, after all. In a world where everybody craves love, he was able to summon it from everyone around him like a snake charmer raising a sleepy cobra from its basket. I can't blame myself for loving him, and I can't regret it either. He betrayed me. But he didn't break me. I'm stronger than I've ever been.

As Will reassures me, "Life is long and complicated. You can live many lives in the course of one." His mother told him that once, he said, and although he didn't really understand at the time, he does now.

It appears Justin lived many lives—as a means of advancement, in order to elicit love, to manipulate, for the sheer, audacious aim of seeing if he could get away with his lies. I plan to live a new life, maybe more than one, but I'm going to take my own sweet time and do it in my own way. I owe that much to myself.

I had hunches and I played them. I was pretty sure Carol had crafted and scheduled Justin's posthumous emails, and she tripped herself up when she told me she didn't know it was possible, as I remembered Justin teaching her how to do it when she moved from New York.

On the other hand, I wasn't 100 percent positive Carol *killed* Justin; the very idea seemed *absurd* on one level. But I kept thinking about that Valium in Justin's system, the pills I'd seen Carol pop on occasion, some of the things she said that just seemed *off*.

I may never know about the car accidents. But I have to wonder. Did Carol tamper with her husband's car or drug him like she did her son? Or was it ten-year-old Justin? Did his close bond with his mother provoke a first act of murderous violence against his father?

And if Justin targeted me at Mammoth, was my own accident there the result of snow and ice or something more sinister? A shiver passes through me just thinking about it.

But there were a few cards I held.

Will's father is very much alive. That performance Will gave at the High Bar? Was just that, a performance. Genius. Who knew Will had it in him?

Porkpie Hat? A professional stuntman that Cousin Lizzie found for us.

And the diners and staff at my dinner with Carol? All police. I may have been fooled, but it turns out I'm not a fool, after all.

A couple of final definitions:

convince [kən-ˈvins]
    verb, cause (someone) to believe firmly in the truth of something

And finally,

From the Glossary of Magic:

Convincer
    a delicate gesture done in order to emphasize a wrong conception, and strengthen the audience's belief in it.

It looks like I am a storyteller in the end. It's no surprise, really. After all, I learned from the very best.

Acknowledgments

When I wrote my first novel, *Just Fall,* it was a "bucket list" item, but I had no expectations (only vague hopes) about actually getting it published. That effort, which began as a private exercise to reclaim a love of craft that was suffering under the vagaries of a Hollywood career, has transformed into a new and glorious chapter of my life. I am humbled by, and grateful for, the steps and missteps throughout my life that have led me to this, my fourth published thriller.

There are many people who have helped me along the way that I need to thank, starting with the team at Ballantine: Kara Welsh, Kim Hovey, Allison Schuster, Madeleine Kenney, Melissa Sanford, Sarah Breivogel, Jesse Shuman, Loren Noveck, Denise Cronin and her team, and last but by no means least my lovely and talented editor, Anne Speyer, who helped me lift this work to the next level.

I'd also like to acknowledge my manager and partner in crime, Darryl Taja.

I have deep appreciation for my team at NYU LA: Daniel Esquivel, Chateau Bezzera, Eric Peterson, and the infinitely resourceful Gracie Corapi. I also need to give a shout out to all of the people at NYU Global Programs for their unwavering support, especially Linda Mills, Nancy Harrison, Dennis Clark, Andrea Gural, Janet Alperstein, Peter Holm, Tyra Liebmann, and Chris Nicolussi.

And then there are my friends and family members, without whom I am essentially useless. This network of support is what keeps me going. My kids, Raphaela and Xander: You are always and ever my two best creations. My husband, Gary: Thank you for getting out of my way when I'm deep in process and for not complaining about that too much. My dad, Ed Sadowsky: You are an inspiration in all ways. A special nod to Janet Cooke, my "publishing whisperer." And blessings and thank-yous to Jonathan Sadowsky, Laura Steinberg, Ivan Sadowsky, Julia Sadowsky, Richard Sadowsky, Mary Clancy, Eric Sadowsky, Katherine Sadowsky, Suzanne Sadowsky, Heather Richardson, Sadie Carter, Josh Carter, Jacob Carter, Arielle Hakman, Daniel Hakman, Darius Margalith, Sean Smith, Rachmil Hakman, Barbara Zerulik, Debbie Hakman, Robin Sax, Kingsley Smith, Laina Cohn, Michelle Raimo, Deb Aquila, Betsy Stahl, Debbie Liebling, Analia Rey, Katrina Kudlick, Tarek Bishara, Mathew Mizel, Sukee Chew, Richard Geddes, Felicia Henderson, Brenda Goodman, Robin Swicord, Wendy Leitman, Lisa Kislak, Shandiz Zandi, Marcy Morris, Melissa Frierichs, Ruth Vitale, Kathy Boluch, Debbie Huffman, Linda Bower, Judy Bloom, Sue Ann Fishkin, Allison Begalman, Sam Rubin, all of those I have inadvertently omitted, and my Bronx High School of Science cohorts (still and always the smartest kids in the room), especially the wonderful Roman Godzich, for his generosity.

ABOUT THE AUTHOR

NINA SADOWSKY is an author, filmmaker, and educator. Her previous novels are *Just Fall, The Burial Society,* and *The Empty Bed*. She has written numerous screenplays and produced such films as *The Wedding Planner*. In addition to her role as program director of NYU Los Angeles, a study away program for advanced students considering careers in the entertainment and media industries, Sadowsky also serves as the director of educational outreach for the Humanitas Prize, is on the leadership committee of Creative Future, and is a founding member of the Woolf Pack, an organization of women showrunners, writers, and producers committed to community and mentorship.

ninasadowsky.com
Facebook.com/ninasadowskythrillers
Twitter: @sadowsky_nina
Instagram: @ninasadowsky

ABOUT THE TYPE

This book was set in Sabon, a typeface designed by the well-known German typographer Jan Tschichold (1902–74). Sabon's design is based upon the original letter forms of sixteenth-century French type designer Claude Garamond and was created specifically to be used for three sources: foundry type for hand composition, Linotype, and Monotype. Tschichold named his typeface for the famous Frankfurt typefounder Jacques Sabon (c. 1520–80).